Faith kept her gaze downward, being mindful of the uneven ground and sharp stones in the Troyers' driveway.

She had taken only a few steps when she bumped into someone. Lifting her head, Faith found herself staring into a pair of the darkest brown eyes she'd ever seen. They were almost black. She shifted her body quickly to the right, but the man with thick brown hair moved to his left at the same time. With a nervous laugh, she swung to the left, just as he transferred his body to the right.

"Sorry. We seem to be goin' the same way," he said with a deep chuckle. There was a small scar in the middle of his chin, and for a moment, Faith thought she recognized him. No, it couldn't be. Noah Hertzler, whom she'd seen fall from the swing on the school playground many years ago, had been left with that kind of scar as a reminder. But this mature man couldn't be the same scrawny teenager Faith had last seen.

"I don't believe we've met," the man said, extending his hand toward Faith. "My name's Noah Hertzler."

"I'm Faith Andrews. . .used to be Stutzman."

Noah's jaw dropped open, and at the same time, Faith felt as if the wind had been knocked clean out of her. A trickle of sweat rolled down her forehead, and she knew it wasn't from the warm summer sun. The man who stood before her was no longer the skinny, red-faced kid, afraid of his own shadow. Instead he was tall, muscular, tanned, and looking at her in a most peculiar way.

"Faith Andrews, the comedian who can yodel?" he asked, lifting his dark eyebrows in obvious surprise.

She nodded and tucked a stray hair behind one ear. "One and the same."

WANDA E. BRUNSTETTER lives in Central Washington with her husband who is a pastor. She has two grown children and six grandchildren. Wanda is a professional ventriloquist and puppeteer and enjoys doing programs for children of all ages. Wanda's greatest joy as an author is writing about the Amish, whose simple lifestyle and commitment to God and family are a reminder of something we all need. Wanda invites you to visit her Web site: www.wandabrunstetter.com

Books by Wanda E. Brunstetter

HEARTSONG PRESENTS
HP254—A Merry Heart
HP421—Looking for a Miracle
HP465—Talking for Two
HP478—Plain and Fancy
HP486—The Hope Chest
HP517—The Neighborly Thing
HP542—Clowning Around
HP579—Kelly's Chance

Don't miss out on any of our super romances. Write to us at the following address for information on our newest releases and club information.

Heartsong Presents Readers' Service
PO Box 719
Uhrichsville, OH 44683

Or visit www.heartsongpresents.com

Going Home

Wanda E. Brunstetter

Heartsong Presents

To all my in-laws living in Pennsylvania, who make "going home" a joyful experience. And to my son-in-law, Bill, who is such a big help in the kitchen.

A note from the Author:
I love to hear from my readers! You may correspond with me by writing:

Wanda E. Brunstetter
Author Relations
PO Box 719
Uhrichsville, OH 44683

ISBN 1-59310-241-0

GOING HOME

Our mission is to publish and distribute inspirational products offering exceptional value and biblical encouragement to the masses.

All scripture quotations are taken from the King James Version of the Bible.

PRINTED IN THE U.S.A.

Or check out our Web site at www.heartsongpresents.com

one

Faith Andrews stared out the bus window, hoping to focus on something other than her immediate need. She feasted her eyes on rocky hills, scattered trees, and a June sky so blue she felt as if she could swim in it. Faith had always loved this stretch of road in her home state of Missouri. She'd traveled it plenty of times over the last ten years, going from Branson to Springfield and back again, doing numerous stage appearances at theaters in both towns. She'd also been in Tennessee, Arkansas, and several other southern states, but her favorite place to entertain was Branson. All the shows in that area were family-oriented, lively and fun. Not like some nightclubs where her husband, who'd also doubled as her agent, had booked her to appear during the early days of her career. Faith hated those gigs, with leering men who sometimes shouted obscene remarks and people asking dumb questions about the getup Greg insisted she wear for a time.

"You need to wear your Amish garb," he'd told her. "It can be your trademark."

Faith shook her head at the remembrance. *Sure glad I finally convinced him it wasn't helping my image, and we decided to go with the hillbilly look instead.*

Whenever Faith was onstage, the past, present, and future disappeared like trees in the forest on a foggy day. When she entertained, her focus was only on one thing—telling jokes and yodeling her heart out for an appreciative audience.

Faith closed her eyes, relishing the vision of a performance she had done six months ago at a small theater in the area

5

known as "Old Branson." Her jokes had brought down the house that night. She liked it when she could make people laugh. Too bad it was a talent that had never been valued until she'd become a professional entertainer. Her family didn't care for humor. Maybe she wouldn't have felt the need to run away if they'd been more accepting of her silliness.

Faith's thoughts took her back to the stage again, as she remembered receiving a standing ovation and basking in the warmth of it even after the theater was empty. How could she have known her world would be turned upside down in a single moment following that program? When Faith took her final bow, she had no idea she would be burying her husband of seven years a few days later or that she would be sitting on a bus right now, heading for home.

Going back to her birthplace outside the town of Seymour, Missouri, was something Faith vowed she would never do. So near, yet so far away, she'd been these last ten years, and never once had she returned for a visit. Not that she would have been welcomed, for she'd been a rebellious teenager, refusing baptism and membership into the Amish church. Since she wasn't a church member, Faith's family and friends wouldn't have officially shunned her, but they surely could have made life miserable if she'd stuck around.

Faith had sent a few notes to her childhood companion Barbara Raber during the first years of her absence, but that was the only contact she'd had with anyone from home. If not for the necessity of finding a stable environment for Melinda, Faith wouldn't be going home now.

She turned away from the window, and her gaze came to rest on the sleeping child beside her. Faith's six-year-old daughter's cheeks had turned rosy as her eyelids closed in slumber soon after they'd boarded the bus in Branson.

Faith smiled at the remembrance of Melinda bouncing

around while they waited in the bus station. "Mommy, I can't wait to get on the bus and go see where you were born."

"I hope you like what you see, my sweet girl," Faith murmured as she studied her daughter. The little girl's head lolled against Faith's arm, and her breathing was sweet and even. Melinda had been sullen since her father's death. Maybe the change of scenery and a different lifestyle would be just what she needed.

Such a beautiful child. So innocent and unsuspecting of what lies ahead. Faith pushed a wayward strand of golden hair away from Melinda's face. She looked a lot like Faith had as a little girl—same blond hair and clear blue eyes, only Melinda wore her hair hanging down her back or in a ponytail. In the Amish community, she would be expected to wear it in a tight braid, curled around the back of her head, then covered with a dark scarf or black prayer *kapp*, the way Faith had done for so many years.

Will Mama and Papa accept my baby girl, even though they might not take kindly to me? Will Melinda adjust to her new surroundings, so plain and devoid of all worldly pleasures? When I'm gone, will she feel as though I've abandoned her?

As Faith took hold of her daughter's small hand, she felt a familiar burning in the back of her throat. She relished the warmth and familiarity of Melinda's soft skin and could hardly fathom what it would be like for the two of them once they were separated. Yet she'd do anything for her child—even that which she'd promised never to do—go back to her Amish community. She was convinced it would be better for Melinda than being hauled all over the countryside with only one parent. She'd been doing that ever since Greg died six months ago, and things hadn't gone well.

Besides the fact that Faith still hadn't secured another agent to book her shows, she'd had a terrible time coming up with a babysitter for Melinda. At times she had to take the child with her to rehearsals and even some shows. Melinda would sit offstage while one of the other performers looked after her as Faith did her routine. Faith had finished up her contract at a theater in Branson last night, and this morning she and Melinda boarded a bus. Faith wouldn't go back to entertaining until she was free to do so, which meant she had to know Melinda was in good hands.

Faith had left her name with a talent agency in Memphis, Tennessee, and given them her parents' address so they could contact her there. She hoped Melinda would have time to adjust to her new surroundings before an agent decided to represent her.

Faith gripped the armrest of her seat on the bus as she thought about her other options. When Greg's parents had come to Branson for his funeral, they'd offered their assistance if needed. "Remember now, Faith," Elsie had said. "If you need anything, give us a call."

Faith figured the offer was made purely out of obligation, for John and Elsie Andrews were too self-centered to care about anyone but themselves. She wasn't about to ask if Melinda could live with Greg's parents. That would be the worst thing possible, even if his folks were willing to take on the responsibility of raising their granddaughter.

Elsie and John lived in Los Angeles, California, and Greg's dad was an alcoholic. Faith had met her husband's parents only once before his death. That was shortly after they'd gotten married. They had stayed with them for one week, while they visited Disneyland, Knott's Berry Farm, and some other sights in the area. It hadn't taken Faith long to realize that Greg's parents weren't fit to raise any child.

Elsie Andrews was a self-centered woman who only cared about her own needs. During their visit, all the woman talked about was her circle of friends and when she was scheduled for her next facial or hair appointment. Greg's dad always seemed to have a drink in his hand, and he used language so foul Faith cringed every time he opened his mouth. Melinda would be better off in Webster County, with her Plain relatives, than she would with grandparents who thought more about alcohol and mudpacks than having a personal relationship with their only son and his wife.

Faith let her eyelids close once more, allowing herself to travel back to when she was a teenager. She saw herself in the barn, sitting on a bale of hay, yodeling and telling jokes to her private audience of two buggy horses and a cat named Boots.

&

"Faith Stutzman, what do you think you're doin'?"

Faith whirled around at the sound of her father's deep voice. His face was a mask of anger, his dark eyebrows drawn together so they almost met in the middle.

"I was entertainin' the animals," she said, feeling her defenses rising. "I don't see any harm in that, Papa."

He scowled at her. "Is that a fact? What about the chores you were sent out here to do? Have ya finished those?"

She shook her head. "Not yet, but I'm aimin' to get them done soon."

Papa nudged her arm with his knuckles. "Then get up and do 'em! And no more of that silly squawkin' and howlin'. You sound like a frog with a sore throat, trying to do that silly yodelin' stuff." He started for the barn door but turned back around. "You've always been a bit of a rebel, and it ain't gettin' no better now that you've reached your teen years." He shook his finger at Faith. "You'd better start spendin' more time reading the scriptures and prayin' and less time in town soakin' up all kinds of worldly stuff on the sly. You'll surely

die in your sins if ya don't get yourself under control and pre-
pare for baptism soon."

When the barn door slammed shut, Faith stuck out her
tongue, feeling more defiant than ever. "I should be allowed
to tell jokes and yodel whenever I choose," she grumbled to
Barney, one of the driving horses. "And I shouldn't have to
put up with Papa's outbursts or his mean, controlling ways."
She plucked a piece of hay from the bale on which she sat
and snapped off the end. "I'll show you, Papa. I'll show
everyone in this family that I don't need a single one of you. I
can be anything I want to be, and I can do whatever I please.
Just wait and see if I don't!"

❧

As Faith's thoughts returned to the present, she tried to focus
her attention on the scenery whizzing past. She couldn't. Her
mind was a jumble of confusion. Was taking Melinda to
Webster County the right thing?

*I'm doing what I have to do. Melinda needs a secure home, and
this is the best way to make that happen.* Faith thought about
Greg and how, even though he wasn't the ideal husband, he
had secured plenty of engagements for her. Never mind that
Greg kept a good deal of the money she had made to support
his drinking and gambling habits. Never mind that he had
been so harsh with her.

It's sad, she mused. *Greg's been gone six months; yet I grieved
for him only a short time. Even then it wasn't really my husband
I missed. It was my agent and the fact that he took care of our
daughter while I was working.*

Faith popped her knuckles. It was a bad habit—her parents had said so often enough—but it helped relieve some of
her tension. *I'll never marry again—that's for certain sure. It
would be hard to trust another man.* She drew in a deep breath
and tried to relax. She'd be home in a few hours and would

know whether she'd made the right decision or not. If her folks accepted Melinda, the grandchild they knew nothing about, Faith could be fairly certain things would work out.

❧

Noah Hertzler wiped his floury hands on a dish towel and smiled to himself. He was alone in the kitchen and had created another pie he was sure would tempt even the most finicky person. Being the youngest of ten boys, with no sisters in the family, Noah had been the only son who had eagerly helped Mom in the kitchen. He enjoyed cooking and baking. In Noah's mind, his ability to cook was a God-given talent—one he enjoyed sharing with others through the breads, cookies, cakes, and pies he often made to give away. If he heard of someone who was emotionally down or physically under the weather, he set right to work baking a scrumptious dessert to give that person. With it he always attached a note that included one of his favorite verses of scripture. "Food for the stomach and nourishment for the soul." That's what Mom called Noah's gifts to others.

Noah stared out the kitchen window into the backyard where he had played as a child. Growing up, he'd been so shy, unable to express his thoughts or feelings the way other children usually did. When his friends or brothers gathered to play, Noah either spent time alone in the barn or helped his mother in the kitchen. Even now, at age twenty-four, he was somewhat reserved and spoke only when he felt something needed to be said. Noah thought it was for this reason he wasn't yet married. The truth was, he'd been too shy to pursue a woman, although he had never found anyone he wanted to court.

Noah figured another reason for his single status was because he wasn't so good-looking. Not that he was ugly, for Mom had often said his thick, mahogany-colored hair and dark brown eyes reminded her of a box of sweet chocolates. Of course, all mothers thought their *kinner* were cute and sweet; it was the way of a good mother's heart to see the best in her children.

Instinctively Noah touched his nose. Despite the good color of his hair and eyes, he thought his nose was too big, and it had a small hump in the middle of it. He'd taken a lot of ribbing from his friends during childhood over that beak. He could still hear his schoolmates chanting, "Noah! Noah! Nobody knows of anything bigger than Noah's huge nose!"

Forcing his thoughts to return to the present, Noah's gaze came to rest on the old glider, which sat under the red-leafed maple tree in their backyard. He had seen many of his brothers share that swing with their sweethearts, but Noah had never had the pleasure. He'd shown an interest in only a few girls since his teen years, and those relationships didn't involve more than a ride home in Noah's open buggy after a young people's singing on a Sunday night. He'd never taken it any further than that because he had been so shy.

Most everyone in the community thought Noah was a confirmed bachelor; some had said so right to his face. But he didn't much care what others thought. Noah was content to work five days a week for Hank Osborn, a local English man who raised Christmas trees. In the evenings and on weekends, Noah helped his mother at home. Mom was sixty-two years old and had been diagnosed with diabetes a few years back. As careful as she was about her diet, her health was beginning to fail. She needed Noah's help now more than ever. Especially since he was the only son still living at home. All nine of Noah's brothers were married, with families of their own. Pap, at age sixty-four, still kept busy with farm chores and raising his fat hogs. He surely didn't have time to help his wife with household chores or cooking. Not that he would have anyway. Noah's dad hated indoor chores, even hauling firewood into the kitchen, which had been Noah's job since he was old enough to hold a chunk of wood in his chubby little hands.

Bringing his reflections to a halt, Noah opened the oven door and slid two pie tins inside, knowing it would take only a few minutes for the shells to turn golden brown. Then he would wait for them to cool before filling each with the mixture he'd put together for Lemon Sponge pie, his favorite dessert. One of the pies would be for him and his folks. The other he planned to give away, as soon as he found someone with a need. Noah had already decided the verse of scripture would be from Hebrews 11:6: "But without faith it is impossible to please him: for he that cometh to God must believe that he is, and that he is a rewarder of them that diligently seek him." Bishop Martin had quoted the verse last Sunday at Preaching, and Noah had been thinking on it ever since.

"Is there someone in the community who's struggling with a lack of faith?" he murmured. "Do they need a reminder that will encourage their heart and help strengthen their trust in God?" If so, Noah felt confident the Lord would direct him to give that person the pie with the verse he planned to attach. He could hardly wait to see who it might be.

&

Holding tightly to Melinda with one hand and clutching their red suitcase with the other, Faith moved toward the pumps when they got off the bus at the gas station in Seymour. The unmistakable aroma of country air assaulted her senses. She was so close to home she could smell it. There was no turning back. She'd come this far; she would go the rest of the way.

Faith didn't recognize the man working at the gas station, but she asked him about hiring someone to drive them to her folks' place. He introduced himself as Ed Moore, said he'd only been living in Seymour two years, then offered his wife's services.

"Doris is comin' by soon and plans to buy some eggs from an Amish farm out thataway," Ed said.

A short time later, his wife showed up and agreed to drive Faith and Melinda to the Stutzmans'. Ed opened the back of Doris's station wagon and deposited their luggage inside. He probably thought it was strange they had only one suitcase between them, but Faith didn't care what the man believed. When she'd decided to make this trip, she left most of their things in a small storage unit in Branson. Where they were going, they needed only the basic necessities, and in case things didn't work out, they wouldn't have a lot of excess baggage to haul off if they left in a hurry.

Faith and Melinda climbed into the backseat of Doris Moore's vehicle, and Faith buckled both their seat belts. "Where are we going, Mommy?" the child asked.

Faith tucked her daughter's white cotton blouse under the band of her blue jeans. "I told you before, honey. We're going to meet your grandparents. We'll be staying with them for a while."

Melinda pressed her nose to the window as the car headed out of town and past the local McDonald's restaurant. Faith noticed an Amish man tying his horse and buggy to the hitching post in front. She guessed some things had changed—at least here in town.

As the station wagon turned onto the country road leading to her parents' home, Melinda pointed out the window. "Look at all the farms. There are so many animals!"

"Your grandma and grandpa Stutzman have all kinds of critters you'll soon get to know," Faith told the child.

Melinda made no comment, and Faith wondered what her

precious girl was thinking. Would her daughter find joy in the things on the farm? She hoped Melinda would adjust to the new surroundings and respond well to her grandparents and other family members.

Closing her eyes, Faith leaned against the upholstered seat and tried to relax. She would deal first with seeing her folks and then worry about how well Melinda could adjust. She only had the strength to work through one problem at a time and was glad Doris didn't seem to mind her sitting in the back with Melinda. It was hard enough to concentrate on what her daughter had to say without trying to make idle talk with a total stranger.

Twenty minutes later, they pulled into the gravel driveway of her parents' farm. Faith opened the car door and stepped out. Letting her gaze travel around the yard, she was amazed at how little it had changed. Everything looked nearly the same as the day she'd left home. The house was still painted white. The front porch sagged on one end. Dark shades hung at each of the windows.

A wagonload of steel milk cans was parked out by the garden, and two open buggies sat near the barn. Her folks' only mode of transportation was obviously the same as it had always been.

Faith shook her head. Did she think it would be any different? Even as a child, she'd never been able to understand why their district adhered to the idea that they must drive only open buggies. Traveling in such a way could be downright miserable when the weather turned cold and snowy. She'd heard it said that the Webster County Amish were the strictest in their beliefs of any Plain community in America. Seeing her parents' simple home again made her believe this statement must be true.

Faith noticed something else. A dark gray, closed-in buggy

was parked on one side of the house. How strange it looked. Her mind whirled with unanswered questions. *I wonder whose it could be. Unless the rules around here have changed, it surely doesn't belong to Papa.*

"Is this the place?" Melinda asked.

She looked down at her daughter, so innocent and wide-eyed. "Yes, honey. This is where Mommy grew up. Shall we go see if anyone's at home?" Melinda nodded, although her clouded expression left little doubt of the child's concerns.

Faith offered to pay Doris Moore, but she waved her away. "No need for that. I was headin' this way anyhow."

Faith thanked the middle-aged woman, grabbed their suitcase, and gulped in another breath of air. It was time to face the music.

two

Faith had only made it to the first step of the front porch when the door swung open. Her mother, Wilma Stutzman, stepped out, and a little girl not much older than Melinda followed. In some ways Mama looked the same, yet she was different. Hair that used to be as blond as spun gold was now dingy and graying. Her skin revealed wrinkles where it had once been smooth and soft. Mama's face looked tired and drawn, and her blue eyes, offset by metal-framed glasses, held no sparkle, as they once had.

"Can I help ya with somethin'?" her mother asked, looking at Faith as though she were a total stranger.

Faith stepped all the way onto the porch, bringing Melinda with her. "Mama, it's me."

The older woman eyed Faith up and down, and her mouth dropped open. Then her gaze came to rest on Melinda, who was clinging to Faith's hand as though her young life hung in the balance.

"Faith?" Mama squeaked. "After all these years, is it really you?"

Faith nodded, as tears stung the backs of her eyes. It was good to see her mother again. "This is my daughter, Mama. Melinda's six years old." Faith gave the child's hand a gentle squeeze. "Say hello to your grandma Stutzman."

"Hello, Grandma." Melinda's voice was barely above a whisper.

Mama's pale eyebrows lifted in obvious surprise, but she offered Melinda a brief smile. Her brows drew together then, as she looked at Faith once more. "I didn't even know you was married, much less had a child. Where have ya been these last ten years?"

Faith swallowed hard as she searched for the right words. "I—uh—followed my dream, Mama."

"What dream? You up and run off the day you turned eighteen, with only a note that said you was leavin' to become part of the English world."

"My dream was to use my yodeling skills and joke-telling to entertain folks. My husband, Greg, made that happen, and I've been on the road entertaining for quite a spell."

Mama's eyes glistened with unshed tears. "It broke your *daed's* and my heart when you left home. Don't ya know that?"

Faith dropped her gaze to the slanting porch. "Greg was killed six months ago when a car hit him." No point telling Mama that her husband had been drinking when he stepped in front of the oncoming vehicle. Mama would probably think Faith also drank liquor, and then she'd most likely receive a stern lecture on the evils of strong drink. She'd had enough of those reprimands during her teen years when she'd been sowing her wild oats.

"I'm sorry about your husband." Mama sounded sincere. Maybe she did care a little bit.

Feeling the need to change the subject, Faith nodded at the gray, closed-in buggy sitting out in the yard. "Mind if I ask who that belongs to?"

"Vernon Miller, the buggy maker. He's out in the barn with your *daed*."

"Does that mean the Webster County Amish are allowed to drive closed-in buggies now?"

Mama shook her head. "Vernon built the Lancaster-style carriage for an English man who lives out in Oregon. The fellow owns a gift shop there, where he sells Amish-made items.

Guess he decided havin' a real buggy in front of his place would be good for business." She shrugged her shoulders. "Vernon wanted to test-drive it before he completed the order and had it sent off."

"I might have known things hadn't changed here," Faith mumbled.

She was going to say more, but the young girl with light brown hair and dark eyes who stood beside Mama spoke up. "Do I know these people, *Mamm*?"

Mamm? Faith felt a jolt of electricity zip through her body. Was the child hanging onto Mama's long blue dress Faith's sister? Had Mama given birth to a baby sometime after Faith left home? Did that mean Faith had three sisters now instead of two? She could have more than four brothers, too, and not even know it.

"Susie, this is your big sister," Mama said to the girl. "And her daughter's your niece."

Susie stood there, gaping at Faith as though she'd grown a set of horns. Was it her worldly attire of blue jeans and a pink T-shirt that bothered the girl? Could it have been the long French braid Faith wore down her back? Or was the child as surprised as Faith over the news that each of them had a sister they knew nothing about?

"So what are you doin' here?" Mama asked, looking back at Faith.

"I—I—was wondering if Melinda and I could stay with you for a while." Faith held her breath and waited for her mother's answer. Would she and Melinda be welcomed or turned away?

"Here? With us?" Mama's voice had risen at least an octave, and her eyes, peering through her glasses, were as huge as saucers.

Faith nodded.

"As English or Amish?"

Her mother's direct question went straight to Faith's heart. If she told the truth—that she wanted her daughter to be Amish, and she would pretend to be until she was ready to leave—the door would probably be slammed in her face.

Faith gnawed on her lower lip, as she considered her response. She had to be careful. It wouldn't be good to reveal her plan until the time was right. "I—uh—am willing to return to the Amish way of life."

"And you'll speak to Bishop Martin yet today, before you attend church with us in the mornin'?"

Faith gulped. She hadn't expected to speak with the bishop on her first day home. She'd probably be subjected to one of his long, firm lectures and told she must confess the error of her ways and be baptized into the church before she would be fully accepted.

Melinda tugged on her hand. "Are we gonna stay here, Mommy?"

"I hope so," Faith replied. They couldn't be turned away. They had no place to go but back on the road, and Faith was through with dragging Melinda all over creation. It wasn't good for a child to live out of a suitcase, never knowing from week to week where she would lay her head at night. Melinda should attend school in the fall, and she needed a stable environment. Faith would endure almost anything to provide a safe haven for her daughter—even subject herself to the reprimanding tongue of their bishop.

"Will ya speak with Jacob Martin or not?" Mama asked again.

Faith gritted her teeth and nodded.

Mama stepped aside and held the screen door open. "Come inside then."

꙰

Noah looked forward to going to Preaching today. The service would be held at his friend Isaac Troyer's place. Isaac and his wife, Emma, had been married four years and had two small children already. Noah enjoyed spending time with other people's *kinner*. He figured that was a good thing, since it wasn't likely he'd ever have any of his own.

"Gotta be married to have kids," Noah muttered as he scrambled a batch of eggs for breakfast.

"Couldn't quite make out what you was sayin', but you were talkin' to yourself again, huh?"

Noah turned at the sound of his mother's voice. He hadn't realized she'd come into the kitchen. "Yeah, I guess so," he admitted, turning to face her.

"You gotta quit doin' that, son." Mom's hazel-colored eyes looked perky this morning, and Noah was glad she seemed to be feeling better. Yesterday she'd been kind of shaky-like.

His mother shuffled over to the gas-operated refrigerator, withdrew a slab of bacon, and handed it to Noah. "Some of your *daed*'s best."

He chuckled. "All of Pap's hogs are the best. At least he thinks so."

Mom's head bobbed up and down, and a few brown hairs, sprinkled with gray, came loose from the bun she wore under her dark head covering. "My Levi would sure enough say so."

"You're right about that. Pap gets up early every mornin', rain or shine, and heads right out to feed his pigs. Truth is, I think he enjoys talkin' to the old sows more'n he does me."

Mom clicked her tongue as she set three plates on the table. "Now don't start with that, Noah. It ain't your *daed*'s fault you don't share his interest in raisin' hogs."

"That's not the problem, Mom, and you know it." Noah grabbed a butcher knife from the wooden block on the cupboard and cut several slices of bacon. Then he slapped them into the frying pan. The trouble between him and Pap went back to when Noah was a young boy. He was pretty sure his dad thought he was a sissy because he liked to cook and help Mom with some of the inside chores. That was really dumb, as far as Noah was concerned. Would a sissy work up a sweat planting a bunch of trees? Would a sissy wear calluses on his hands from pruning, shaping, and cutting the Christmas pines English people in the area bought every December?

Mom went back to the refrigerator and took out a container of fresh goat's milk. "Let's talk about somethin' else, shall we? Your *daed* will be in soon from his chorin', and I don't want you all riled up when he gets here."

Noah snorted and flipped the sizzling bacon. "I ain't riled, Mom. Just statin' facts as I see 'em."

"*Jah*, well, you have a right to your opinion."

"Glad you think so. Now if you want to hear more about what I think—"

"Your *daed* loves you, Noah, and that's the truth of it," his mother interrupted.

Noah nodded. "I know, and I love him, too. I also realize Pap doesn't like it because I'd rather be in the kitchen than out sloppin' hogs with him."

Mom sighed. "None of my boys ever enjoyed the pigs the way that husband of mine seems to."

Noah decided it was now time for a change of subject. "I baked a couple of Lemon Sponge pies while you and Pap went to town yesterday. One with sugar and one without."

"You aimin' to give one away or set both out on the table at the meal after Preachin'?"

Noah pushed the bacon around in the pan, trying to get it to brown up evenlike. "Thought I'd give the pie made with sugar to someone who might need a special touch today."

"Guess God will show you who when the time is right."

"*Jah*. That's how it usually goes."

Mom sniffed deeply. "I just hope ya don't develop baker's asthma from workin' around flour so much."

Noah snickered. "I don't think you have to worry none. That usually only happens to them that work in bakeries and such. One would have to be around flour a whole lot more than me to develop baker's asthma."

Pap entered the kitchen just as Noah was dishing up the bacon and scrambled eggs. Noah's dad had dark brown hair, with close-set eyes that matched in color, but his beard had been nearly gray since his late fifties. Now Pap was starting to show his age in other areas, too. His summer-tanned face was creased with wrinkles, he had dark splotches on his hands and arms, and he walked with a much slower gait these days.

"Somethin' smells mighty good this mornin'," Pap said, sniffing the air. "Must have made bacon."

Noah's mother laughed and pointed to the platter full of bacon and eggs. "Our son has outdone himself again, Levi. He made sticky buns, too." She nodded toward the plate in the center of the table, piled high with rolls. Noah had learned to make many sweet treats using a sugar substitute so Mom could enjoy them without affecting her diabetes.

"You takin' the leftover sticky buns to Preachin'?" his dad asked as he washed his hands at the sink.

"Nope. I made a couple of Lemon Sponge pies to take along."

Papa smacked his lips. "Sounds *gut* to me."

Noah smiled to himself. His dad might not like him spending so much time in the kitchen, but he sure did enjoy the fruits of his labor. And Pap never said one word about Noah not helping out with the hogs this morning. Maybe it was a good sign. This might be the beginning of a great day.

Faith felt as fidgety as a bumblebee on a hot summer day. She hadn't been this nervous since the first time she performed one of her comedy routines in front of a bunch of strangers. She and Melinda were sitting in the back of her parents' open buggy, along with young Susie. Faith's other two sisters, Grace, age seventeen, and Esther, who was fourteen, had ridden to church with their brothers, John and Brian. Faith had learned last night that her twenty-four-year-old brother John was courting a woman named Phoebe. Brian, age twenty-two, said he was still looking for the right girl. Faith couldn't believe how much her younger siblings had changed in the ten years since she left home. The boys were adults now, and Grace and Esther weren't far behind. She was shocked when Mama informed her that James and Philip, both in their thirties, were now married and each had four children of their own. Faith knew she wouldn't be seeing them at Preaching today because they'd recently moved up north near Jamesport. But she would be meeting others in their congregation, not to mention facing Bishop Martin again.

Thinking about the bishop caused Faith to reflect on her conference with him yesterday evening. Papa had driven her over to the bishop's house, where she'd been forced to say some things she didn't really mean. She'd heard it said that confession was good for the soul, but her declaration of guilt hadn't been heartfelt; therefore, it had done nothing for Faith's soul except make her feel more resentful. She felt as if she were being forced to submit to rules she didn't believe in. But it wouldn't be forever. Soon she could go back to her life as an entertainer, and then she'd be happy and carefree.

You won't have your daughter with you, her conscience reminded her. *Can you ever be truly happy without Melinda?* Faith shook her head, as though the action might clear away the troubling thoughts. She wouldn't think about that now. She would deal with leaving Melinda when the time came. For now, Faith's only need was to make everyone in her Amish community believe she had come home to stay.

Soon they were pulling into the Troyers' yard, and Faith looked around in amazement. Isaac Troyer's house and barn were enormous, and a huge herd of dairy cows grazed in the pasture nearby. Papa had mentioned something about the Troyers' dairy farm and said it was doing right well.

Faith let her mind wander back to the time when she had attended the one-room schoolhouse not far down the road. As she recalled, Isaac Troyer, her brother John, and Noah Hertzler had all been friends in those days. She remembered Noah as being the shy one of the group. Faith could still see his face turning as red as a radish over something one of the students at school had said. He hardly spoke more than two words, and then it was only if someone talked to him first. Noah wasn't outspoken or full of wisecracks, the way Faith had always been. She'd have to watch her mouth now that she was back home. Jokes and fooling around wouldn't be appreciated, she was sure.

I wonder if Noah's still around, and if so, is the poor man as shy as he used to be?

"You gettin' out or what?"

Faith jerked her head at the sound of her father's deep voice. He leaned against the buggy, his dark eyes looking ever so serious. Papa was a tall, muscular man, and his brown hair and beard were peppered with gray. He was a hard worker who farmed for a living, and he could be equally hard when it came to his family. As a little girl, Faith had always been a bit afraid of him. She wasn't sure if it was his booming voice or his penetrating eyes. One thing for sure, Faith knew Papa would take no guff from any of his children. The way he was looking at her right now made Faith wonder if he could tell what was on her mind. Did he know how much she dreaded going to church this morning?

Faith stepped down from the buggy and turned to help Melinda and Susie out. Chattering like magpies, the little girls, both dressed in traditional Amish clothes, ran toward the Troyers' house. Since Grace and Esther had ridden to church with their older brothers, they were probably off visiting with their friends. Faith was left to walk alone, and as she headed toward the house, she was overcome by the feeling that she was marching into a den of hungry lions. What if she wasn't accepted? What if she said or did something wrong?

She glanced down at her unadorned, dark green dress, on loan from her sister Grace, who was close to Faith in height and weight. She felt plain and unattractive with her hair pulled back in a bun and a dark prayer *kapp* secured to the top of her head. Black head coverings were traditional for Webster County Amish women, but Faith felt conspicuous, not traditional. It felt odd to wear such plain clothes again, and she wondered if she looked as phony on the outside as she knew she was on the inside.

Melinda hadn't seemed to mind putting on one of Aunt Susie's simple dresses. She'd even made some comment about it being fun to play dress-up today.

Oh, to be young again. I hope Melinda keeps her cheerful attitude in the days ahead. Faith kept her gaze downward, being mindful of the uneven ground and sharp stones in the Troyers' driveway. She had taken only a few steps when she bumped into someone. Lifting her head, Faith found herself staring into a pair of the darkest brown eyes she'd ever seen. They were almost black. She shifted her body quickly to the right, but the man with thick brown hair moved to his left at the same time. With a nervous laugh, she swung to the left, just as he transferred his body to the right.

"Sorry. We seem to be goin' the same way," he said with a deep chuckle. There was a small scar in the middle of his chin, and for a moment, Faith thought she recognized him. No, it couldn't be. Noah Hertzler, whom she'd seen fall from the swing on the school playground many years ago, had been left with that kind of scar as a reminder. But this mature man couldn't be the same scrawny teenager Faith had last seen.

"I don't believe we've met," the man said, extending his hand toward Faith. "My name's Noah Hertzler."

"I'm Faith Andrews. . .used to be Stutzman."

Noah's jaw dropped open, and at the same time, Faith felt as if the wind had been knocked clean out of her. A trickle of sweat rolled down her forehead, and she knew it wasn't from the warm summer sun. The man who stood before her was no longer the skinny, red-faced kid, afraid of his own shadow. Instead he was tall, muscular, tanned, and looking at her in a most peculiar way.

"Faith Andrews, the comedian who can yodel?" he asked, lifting his dark eyebrows in obvious surprise.

She nodded and tucked a stray hair behind one ear. "One and the same."

three

Noah could hardly believe Faith Stutzman, rebellious Amish girl turned comedian, was standing in front of him dressed like all the other Plain women who'd come to Preaching this morning. Only, Faith was different. She didn't have the same humble, submissive appearance most Amish women had. Her eyes were the clearest blue, like fresh water flowing from a mountain stream. There was something about the way those eyes flashed—the way she held her head. She seemed proud and maybe a bit haughty. Not the kind of image the other women in his community portrayed. Even though she was wearing plain clothes, Faith Stutzman Andrews was dazzling.

"What are you doin' here?"

"You know about me being a comedian?"

They'd both spoken at the same time, and Noah chuckled. "You go first."

She lifted her chin. "No, you."

She was not only beautiful but feisty, too. Noah conceded to her request. "I—I'm surprised to see you. How long have ya been home?"

"We arrived yesterday afternoon."

"We?" Noah glanced around, thinking a husband or boyfriend must have accompanied Faith.

"My daughter, Melinda, is with me," Faith explained. "My husband died six months ago."

Noah sucked in his breath as he allowed himself to feel her pain. "I'm sorry for your loss."

28

She stared down at her black shoes. *"Danki."*

He wouldn't press her for details. Maybe another time—when they got to know each other better. "It's your turn now."

Her head came up. "Huh?"

"You started to ask a question a few minutes ago. About me knowin' you were a comedian."

"Oh, yeah. I'm surprised you knew. I obviously didn't become a professional entertainer while I was still Amish." Faith pursed her perfectly shaped lips, and he forced himself not to stare at them. "I didn't know Amish men were so aware of what was going on in the modern world."

"My boss is an English man. He often plays tapes, or we listen to his portable radio while we work." Noah smiled, feeling more relaxed than he had in a long time around any woman other than his mother. Usually he got all red in the face and tongue-tied when he tried to make conversation with the opposite sex. "I've heard you perform several times."

She tipped her head to one side. "And you lived to tell about it?"

"You have a wonderful nice way with words. Makes a body laugh, that's for sure." He nodded. "And you can yodel real good, too."

"You think so?"

"Sure. When I was a boy and came over to your place to spend time with John, your silliness and joke-tellin' used to crack me up."

Faith grinned up at him, and his heart skipped a beat. *It must be the deep dimples in her cheeks that make her look so cute when she smiles.*

"Do you really believe I have a talent to make people laugh?"

"I sure do."

She stood straighter, pushing her shoulders back. "That part of my life is over. I've returned to my birthplace so my daughter can have a real home."

"Not because you missed your family and friends?"

She shrugged. "Sure, that, too."

Noah had a funny feeling Faith wasn't being completely honest with him. He was fairly intuitive, and her tone of voice told him she might be hiding something. He didn't think now was the time or place to be asking her a bunch of personal questions, though. Maybe he would have that chance later. He glanced around and noticed his friend Isaac watching him from where he stood over near the barn. Knowing Isaac, Noah figured he would be expected to give a full account of all he and Faith had said to each other.

"I'd better go, since church will be starting soon. Sure is nice to see you again," Noah said. "I hope it works out for you and your daughter."

"I hope so, too. Things are a little strained for us right now. It's going to be a difficult adjustment, I'm sure."

"Ball wollt's besser geh."

She nodded. "Yes, I hope it will soon go better."

Faith walked off toward the house, and Noah headed over to see Isaac. If he didn't, the nosy fellow would most likely seek him out.

"Who was that woman you were talkin' to?" Isaac asked as soon as Noah stepped up beside him. "You two looked pretty cozylike, but I didn't recognize her."

"It was Faith Stutzman, and we weren't cozy," Noah said.

Isaac's dark eyebrows shot up. "Faith Stutzman? The wayward daughter of Menno and Wilma Stutzman?"

"Yep. Her husband died awhile ago, and she and her daughter have moved back home."

"Hmm. . . Seems a might strange to me, what with her bein' gone so long and all." Isaac reached up to scratch the back of his head that was covered with a thick thatch of light brown hair. In the process, he nearly knocked his black felt hat to the ground, but he righted it in time.

"I agree it does seem a bit odd, but then it's really none of my business."

Isaac nudged Noah with his elbow. "So how'd ya happen to strike up a conversation with her?"

"We sort of bumped into each other."

"Did you get all tongue-tied and turn red in the face?"

Noah clenched his teeth. Why did his best friend always try to get the better of him? Isaac had been doing it ever since they were *kinner.* Of course, Noah knew it was just Isaac's way and he wasn't trying to be mean or anything. The man was about as curious as a cat and nothing but a big tease.

"To tell ya the truth, I didn't feel one bit nervous or shy in Faith's presence."

"Right. And pigs can fly," Isaac said with a snicker.

"It's the truth. I didn't stutter or turn red either."

"Oh, oh. That's not a good sign."

"What's that supposed to mean?"

Isaac pounded Noah on the back. "It means if you aren't careful you could end up *mit Lieb* for that woman."

"I ain't gonna be with love," Noah scoffed. "Now quit your kiddin' around."

"I will for now, because church is about to begin." Isaac motioned toward the house, where several people were already filing in through the open doorway.

"Guess we'd better get in there," Noah said, feeling a sense of relief. For the next three hours, he wouldn't have to answer to anyone but the Lord. He could spend his time praying, singing, and reflecting on God's holy Word.

As Noah and his friend moved toward the house, Noah made a decision. He knew now whom he should give the extra Lemon Sponge pie to. The scripture verse he'd attached was about having faith in God, so it seemed appropriate to present it to a woman whose name was Faith. Besides, it would be like a welcome-home gift to someone who reminded him of the prodigal son.

❧

No matter how she tried, Faith could not find a comfortable position. She'd forgotten how hard these backless wooden benches could be. And to think she was going to have to endure this torture for three whole hours! She glanced down at Melinda, who was sitting between her and Susie. How well would her daughter manage during the long, boring service?

Faith's mind wandered, taking her back in time. Back to when she was a little girl, trying not to fidget during one of the bishop's long-winded sermons or lengthy prayers. She'd been taken to the woodshed for a sound *bletching* on more than one occasion, which only added to her discomfort while sitting on the unyielding bench.

If I'm finding it hard to sit still, how could I fault Melinda for getting a bit wiggly? Faith was glad she'd thought to bring a basket filled with some snack foods, in case her daughter got hungry. She'd also allowed Melinda to bring along her favorite toy, even though Grandma Stutzman had frowned on it, saying it wasn't a faceless doll and should be thrown out because it was worldly looking. The doll was vinyl, with long, red hair and bright blue open-and-close eyes. She was dressed in a beautiful purple gown, and Melinda called her "Princess."

How could I make my little girl get rid of the gift her daddy gave her last year on her birthday? Greg might not have been the ideal husband, but I know he cared for Melinda, and she loved him, too. The doll stays, and I'm glad I stood up to Mama and said so. I've atoned for my sins to the bishop, and I'll abide by the Ordnung while I'm living under my parents' roof, but I won't shatter all that's dear to Melinda. Not to appease anyone.

As the service dragged on, Faith became more and more restless. She kept glancing out the living room window, wishing for the freedom to be outside where she could enjoy the pleasant summer day. She knew they would be going outdoors for their noon meal after the service, but that was still a ways off. Besides, she would be expected to serve the men their food before she could relax and enjoy hers. It wasn't fair. She shouldn't have to subject herself to all this in order to provide Melinda with a stable home. If only Greg hadn't died. If only he'd been a better husband.

Faith's negative thoughts drove her on and on, down a not-so-pleasant memory lane. She'd struggled on her own the first years after she left home and had ended up waiting tables and performing on a makeshift stage for a time. Then Greg came along and swept Faith off her feet. He'd said she was talented and could go far in the world of entertainment. Greg's whispered honeyed words and promises had been like music to her ears, and she'd succumbed to his charms.

Faith thought she'd been in love with Greg during the early part of their marriage and had believed the feelings were mutual. Maybe they had been at first, but then Greg began to use her in order to gain riches. The more successful she became as an entertainer, the more of her money he spent on alcohol and games of chance. She suspected he thought she didn't know what he was up to, but Faith was no dummy. She knew exactly why Greg often sank into depression or became hostile toward her. Never Melinda, though. Greg had always been kind to their child.

Of course, he might not have remained docile toward Melinda if he'd lived and kept on drinking the way he was, Faith reminded herself. *If he could smack me around, then what's to say he wouldn't have eventually taken his frustrations out on our daughter?*

"And now, as many of you may already know, one of our

own, who has lived among the English for the last several years, returned to the flock yesterday. We welcome Faith Stutzman and her daughter, Melinda, to our congregation."

Bishop Martin's bellowing voice drove Faith's thoughts to the back of her mind, and she sat up a bit straighter. She glanced around the room, feeling an urgency to escape but knowing she couldn't. All eyes seemed to be focused on her. Many nodded their heads, some smiled, and others merely looked at her with curious stares. What were they thinking? Did everyone see her as a wayward woman who had come crawling home because she had no other place to go? Well, it was true in a sense. She did have nowhere else to go. At least no place she wanted to take Melinda. If she had kept the child on the road with her, it was only a matter of time before her innocent daughter fell prey to some gold digger like her father had been. Faith desired better things for her little girl. She wanted Melinda to know that when she woke up every morning, there would be food on the table and a warm fire to greet her. She needed her precious child to go to bed at night feeling a sense of belonging and that she was nurtured and loved.

You had all those things when you were growing up, the voice in her head reminded her. Faith shook the thoughts aside as she forced herself to concentrate on the bishop's closing prayer. Better to focus on his words than to think of all she'd given up when she left home. She had done it to prove to herself and to her family that she didn't have to do what anyone else said. Faith was her own person, and she'd been blessed with a talent for yodeling and joke-telling, so why shouldn't she use her gift for personal gain?

A rustle of skirts and the murmur of voices made Faith realize the service was over. She glanced around. Everyone was exiting the room. She hadn't even heard the bishop's final "amen." So much for keeping her focus on his prayer.

Faith saw to it that her daughter was in the care of her sister Esther, who was also overseeing little Susie. Then Faith excused herself to go to the kitchen, where several women and teenage girls were scurrying about, trying to get the meal served up as quickly as possible.

"What can I do to help?" she asked Mama, who stood at the cupboard cutting radishes and other fresh vegetables.

Before her mother could respond, Emma Troyer spoke up. "Why don't ya help David Zook's wife serve coffee to the menfolk?" She handed Faith a pot full of hot coffee. "It's real *gut* to have you back among the people. You've been missed."

"*Danki*," Faith said, feeling the need to let her hostess know she was part of the community again. No good could come from letting anyone know her true feelings. She would need to remember to speak their native language when talking to those in the community and especially to obey all the rules and act attentive in church. If Melinda could sit still like a statue, the way she had today, then Faith could certainly do whatever it took to convince her family and friends she had changed and was reconciled with the church.

Smiling at Emma, whom she remembered as being a few years younger than she, Faith accepted the coffeepot. Then she turned and headed out the back door.

The yard was full of wooden tables, and at each one sat a group of men, old and young alike. Faith noticed a dark-haired woman serving coffee at one of the tables. *That must be David Zook's wife.*

She approached the lady, whose back was to her. "Which tables are yet to be served?" she questioned.

The woman turned around, and a slow smile spread across her face. "*Ach, my!* Faith, I'm so happy to see you!"

"Barbara Raber?"

"It's Zook now. I've been married to David for close to five years already." Barbara smiled. "Remember David? He was a year ahead of us in school."

Faith wasn't sure what to say next. She and Barbara had been friends during the years they were growing up. But Faith had scarcely thought about her childhood friend for some time, and she barely remembered a fellow named David Zook.

"It's nice to see you again." Faith's voice sounded formal and strained, even to her own ears. She couldn't help it; she felt formal and strained around everyone here today. Everyone except Noah Hertzler, that is. She had actually enjoyed their brief conversation, and she'd been much more at ease with him than she was right now. It made no sense. She'd hardly known Noah when they were growing up, as he was four years younger than she was. He'd been John's friend, not hers. He had also been shy among strangers back then, and he hadn't said more than a few words to anyone in their family except John. Today, however, Noah seemed confident and easy to talk to.

Almost too easy, she reminded herself. *I'll be leaving here soon, so I can't afford to let myself form any friendships or attachments.* Faith knew she would even have to distance herself from Melinda once the child became adjusted to her new surroundings. It was the only way she'd be able to leave without either of them falling apart. Of course, Faith was sure her emotions would probably crumble like clay as soon as she left. Life without her little girl would not be easy, but it was for the best.

"Faith. Did you hear what I said?"

Barbara's soft-spoken voice and gentle nudge drove Faith's disconcerting thoughts aside.

"What was that?"

"I said, 'I'm glad you've come home.' "

Faith forced herself to smile. "*Danki.*"

"Now about the tables needing to be served—you can take those four on the left." Barbara nodded toward the ones she was referring to.

"Okay." Faith moved quickly away, thinking how much her friend had changed.

Barbara Raber had been slender as a reed when they were teenagers. Barbara Zook was slightly plump, especially around the middle. The mischief that could be seen in young Barbara's eyes had been replaced with a look of peace and contentment. For that, Faith felt a twinge of envy. In all her twenty-eight years, she'd never known true peace or contentment. She had always wanted something she couldn't have. Something more—something better. She'd thought her career as a comedian would bring both things, but it hadn't. Being an entertainer had given Faith a sense of accomplishment, but something always seemed to be missing. Maybe she would find it when she went back on the road.

Faith avoided eye contact as she served the men. She couldn't bear to see any looks of reprimand or even desire, as she had often encountered when she was performing. Men wanted only one thing—to control a woman, and that included not only her body but her soul, as well. First, Papa had made all her decisions, and then Greg took over. It wasn't fair, and she would never allow it to happen again.

As she poured coffee into the last cup at the table, Faith felt a gentle but calloused hand touch her arm. "*Danki.*"

"You're welcome," she murmured, daring to seek out the man's face. It was Noah Hertzler, and his tender expression was nearly her undoing.

"I have somethin' for you," he said quietly. "It's inside, in the refrigerator."

She tipped her head in question. *Why would Noah have*

anything for me? He hardly knows me, and I'm sure he didn't know I'd be here today.

"Go to the kitchen, and I'll meet you there in a few minutes," he whispered.

Faith nodded mutely and moved away. She walked back to the house, feeling like a marionette with no control over its movements.

Relief swept over Faith when she stepped into the kitchen and found no one else there. All the other women must be outside serving the men their meal.

She pulled out a wooden chair and dropped into it. When she placed her hands on the table, Faith noticed they were shaking. *What's wrong with me? I've faced tougher crowds than the one here today, and I didn't feel half as intimidated. I used to make an audience howl and beg for more, even when I was dying on the inside because of the way things were with Greg and me. Yet here, among my people, I can barely even crack a smile.*

Faith squeezed her eyes shut, wishing she remembered how to pray. If she had, she would have asked Jesus to calm her spirit.

When the back door creaked open, Faith jumped. She turned her head to the right.

Noah stood in the doorway with that easygoing grin on his face.

She swallowed hard. What did he have for her? What did he want in return?

Noah closed the door and strolled over to the refrigerator. He opened it and took out a pie, which he set on the table in front of Faith. "This is for you."

"You're giving the whole thing to me?" Faith knew her mouth was hanging wide open, and her eyes probably revealed surprise, as well.

Noah nodded. "It's a Lemon Sponge pie, and I made it

yesterday with the idea of givin' it away today."

"Why me?"

His face flooded with color. "Just call it a welcome-home gift." He pushed the pie pan toward her. "Sure hope you like lemon."

She nodded. "It's one of my favorite flavors."

"That's *gut.* I hope you'll enjoy every bite, as well as the verse of scripture."

Verse of scripture? Faith's gaze went to the little card attached to the side of the pan where Noah pointed. Her heart clenched. She would take the pie, but she had no plans to read that verse!

four

"What have ya got there?" Mama asked, as Faith climbed down from the buggy behind Melinda and Susie.

Noah had placed the pie inside a small cardboard box before he and Faith left the Troyers' kitchen, and Faith had taken it out to the buggy, where she'd slipped it under the backseat. She didn't want to carry it around all day or offer to share it with anyone during the dessert part of their meal. There would have been too many questions. Did Faith bake the pie? If not, then who had? Any number of queries could have been hurdled at her, and she didn't want to answer anyone.

Looking down at the dessert now, Faith hoped it hadn't spoiled. She'd draped a cold cloth over the top and placed a chunk of ice from the Troyers' propane refrigerator in the box to keep it cool. She still wondered why Noah Hertzler had chosen her to be the recipient of his luscious-looking confection.

"Faith? Did ya hear what I asked?"

Clutching the box to her chest, she faced her mother. "It's a Lemon Sponge pie."

Mama's eyebrows arched upward. "Really? Where'd ya get it?"

Faith drew in a deep breath. She may as well get the inquisition over with, because she was sure her mother wouldn't be satisfied until she'd heard all the details. "Noah Hertzler gave it to me."

Mama chuckled softly. "I thought as much. That young fellow is always handin' out his baked goods to someone in our community. Ida Hertzler is one lucky *mamm* to have him for a son; he's right handy in the kitchen.

"Is that so?"

"Yep. From what Ida's told me, Noah's been helpin' out with the cookin' and bakin' ever since he was a *kinner*."

Faith hadn't known that. The only thing she'd ever learned about Noah was that he used to be shy and kind of awkward. He sure didn't seem so today, though.

"Noah's not married, ya know," Mama said as they headed for the house.

Faith figured as much since she hadn't seen him with a woman. It didn't concern her, however, so she made no response to her mother's comment.

"Maybe after you've settled in here and gotten right with the church, you and Noah might hit it off."

Faith whirled around to face her mother. "Mama, Greg's been dead only a short while. It wouldn't be proper for me even to think about another man right now, in case that's what you're insinuating." She sniffed. "Besides, I'm not planning to remarry—ever."

Mama gave her a curious look, but Faith hurried to the house before her mother could say anything more. She didn't want to talk about her disastrous marriage to Greg or the plans she had for the future. Faith figured Mama would probably bring the subject up again, and she would need to be ready with some good answers.

❧

In the days that followed, Faith and Melinda settled into a routine. Faith got up early every morning to help with breakfast, milk the cows, and feed the chickens. She labored from sunup to sunset, taking time out only for meals and to help Melinda learn the traditional Pennsylvania Dutch language of the Amish religion.

The child had also been assigned several chores to do, and she seemed a bit unsure of herself. Melinda acted as if she was all right with the idea of wearing her aunt Susie's plain clothes, but she wasn't used to having so many responsibilities placed on her shoulders. Nor was she accustomed to being taught a foreign language. An Amish child grew up speaking their native tongue, only learning English when they entered school in the first grade. Since Melinda would be starting school in the fall and already spoke English, her task was to learn Pennsylvania Dutch.

"I don't like it here, Mommy. I'm not happy," Melinda whined, as she handed Faith a freshly laundered towel to be hung on the clothesline that was situated next to the house. "When can we go home?"

Home? They really had no home. Hotels and motels in whatever city Faith was performing in—those were the only homes Melinda had ever known.

Faith clipped the towel in place and patted the top of her daughter's head. "This is our home now, sweetie. Soon you'll get used to the way things are."

Melinda lifted her chin and frowned. "Grandma Stutzman is mean. She makes us both work hard. Aren't you sick of it?"

Of course Faith was sick of it, but she couldn't let the child know that. Faith wasn't used to manual labor anymore, and every muscle in her body ached. In the past few weeks, she'd pulled so many weeds from the garden that her fingers felt stiff and unyielding. Heaps of clothes had been washed and ironed, and she'd helped with the cooking and cleaning and done numerous other chores she was no longer accustomed to doing.

It wasn't the hard work that bothered Faith the most, though. It was the suffocating feeling that she couldn't be herself. She desperately wanted to sit on the porch in the evenings and yodel to her heart's content. She would enjoy telling some jokes or humorous stories and have her family appreciate them.

"Mommy, are you thinkin' about what I said?"

Melinda's question caught Faith's attention. "Everyone in the family has a job to do," she said patiently. "In time we'll get used to it."

The child didn't say anything as she handed another towel to her mother, but Faith could see by her daughter's scowl that she wasn't happy.

"How would you like to eat lunch down by the pond today?" Faith asked, hoping to cheer Melinda up. She had to do something to help her daughter see that living here wasn't all bad.

Melinda's blue eyes lit up. "Can Aunt Susie come, too?"

"If Grandma says it's all right."

"Can we bring our dolls along?"

"If you want to."

There was a brief pause, as Melinda handed Faith a pair of Grandpa Stutzman's trousers to hang on the line. "How come only the men wear pants here?"

"Grandpa and Grandma belong to the Amish faith, and the church believes only men and boys should wear pants," Faith explained.

Melinda's forehead wrinkled. "Does that mean I ain't never gonna wear jeans again?"

"I'm not ever," Faith corrected.

Melinda nodded soberly. "You and me ain't never gonna wear pants."

Faith swallowed back a chuckle, as she knelt on the grass and touched the hem of Melinda's unadorned blue cotton frock. "I thought you liked wearing dresses."

"Sometimes I do, but I also like to wear pants."

"You'll get used to wearing only dresses." Even as the

words slipped off her tongue, Faith wondered if her prediction would come true. She'd seen what English children were allowed to wear and had never gotten used to the strict dress code she had been expected to adhere to during her growing-up years. Was it fair to require her daughter to do the things she had always resented?

"Here's the last towel, Mommy. Now can I go swing?"

"Maybe after lunch." Faith couldn't believe how quickly Melinda had changed the subject. She no longer seemed concerned about not wearing jeans, and her thoughts had turned to play. Maybe the child would adjust after all. She seemed to enjoy many things here on the farm—spending time with Aunt Susie, playing with a batch of new kittens, swinging on the same wooden swing Faith had used when she was a little girl. In time, maybe Melinda would learn to be content with everything about her new life as an Amish girl. In the meantime, Faith would try to make her daughter feel as secure as possible and show her some of the good things about being Plain.

Faith was determined to make this work for Melinda and equally determined to get back on the road as soon as possible. Mama was already pressing her about being baptized and joining the church. Faith didn't know how much longer she could put it off, but for now she'd convinced her mother she needed more time to adjust to the Amish way of life. She'd been gone a long time and couldn't be expected to change overnight. Not that she planned to change. Whenever Faith had a few moments alone, she would practice her yodeling skills and tell a few jokes to whatever animal she might be feeding. Soon she would be onstage again, wearing her hillbilly costume and entertaining an approving audience. Around here no one appreciated anything that wasn't related to hard work.

Faith hung the last article of clothing on the line, picked up the wicker basket, and took hold of Melinda's hand. As much as she wanted to be far away from Webster County, Faith knew she couldn't leave her daughter practically among strangers while she ran off to do her own thing. She had to stay awhile longer—to be sure Melinda was accepted, and so she could know the child had adjusted well enough to her new surroundings. Besides, she hadn't heard from the talent agency yet. Without an agent, her career would go nowhere. On her own, all she could hope for were one-night stands and programs in small theaters that didn't pay nearly as well as the bigger ones did.

"Let's go to the kitchen and see what we can make for our picnic lunch, shall we?" Faith suggested.

The child nodded eagerly, and the soft *ma–a* of a nearby goat caused them both to laugh as they skipped along the path leading to the house. On the way they tromped through a mud puddle made by the rain that had fallen during the night. Faith felt the grimy mud ooze between her bare toes. She'd almost forgotten what it was like to go barefoot every summer. It wasn't such a bad thing, really. Especially on the grass, so soft and cushy.

It was good to laugh and let her hair down. *What a shame I can't really let it down*, Faith mused, as she considered the dark head scarf covering the bun she wore at the back of her head. The only time Faith's long hair was let down anymore was when she went to bed or washed it during a bath.

When Faith and Melinda entered the kitchen, they were greeted with a look of disapproval from Faith's mother. "*Ach, my!* Your feet are muddy. Can't ya see I just cleaned the floor?"

Faith looked down at the grubby footprints they'd created. "Sorry, Mama. We'll go back outside and clean the dirt off our feet." She grabbed Melinda's hand and scooted her out the door.

"I told you Grandma Stutzman is mean," Melinda said with tears in her eyes. "She's always hollerin' about somethin'."

"It might seem so, but Grandma just wants to keep her kitchen clean." Faith led her daughter over to the water trough and lifted, then pushed the handle on the pump up and down. She washed their feet, drying them with a towel she had grabbed off the kitchen counter before they'd gone out the back door.

"Can we still take our lunch down by the pond?" Melinda questioned.

"Sure, honey."

"And Susie can come, too?"

"If Grandma says it's all right."

Melinda's lower lip protruded. "She'll probably say no, 'cause she's in a bad mood 'bout us trackin' in mud."

"I don't think she'll make Susie pay for our transgressions."

"Our what?"

"Transgressions. It means doing wrong things."

Melinda hung her head. "I always seem to be doin' wrong things around here. I must be very bad."

Faith knelt on the ground and pulled her daughter into her arms. "You're not bad. You just don't understand all the rules yet."

"Will I ever, Mommy?"

Faith stroked the child's cheek. "Of course you will. It's just going to take a little more time."

Guilt found its way into Faith's heart and put down roots so deep she thought she might choke. She'd never accepted the rules when she was growing up. She'd experimented with modern things whenever she had the chance and therefore had never fully accepted the Amish way of life. Had it really been all those rules that drove her away, or was it the simple fact that she'd never felt truly loved and acknowledged?

❧

Noah whistled in response to the call of a finch as he knelt in front of a newly planted pine tree. It was still scrawny compared to those around it, and the seedling appeared to be struggling to survive.

"A little more time and attention are what you're needin'," he whispered, resolving to save the fledgling. He wanted to see it thrive and someday find its way to one of the local Christmas tree lots or be purchased by someone who would come to the farm to choose their own holiday tree.

The sound of country-western music blared in his ear, and Noah knew his boss, Hank Osborn, must be nearby. Hank enjoyed listening to the radio while he worked, and Noah had discovered he rather liked it, too. Of course, he'd not let his folks or anyone from their community know that. They would probably disapprove and think he'd gone worldly on them.

Noah didn't believe there was anything wrong with listening to the radio, and he'd never do it on his own. But here at work, it was kind of nice. Besides, this was his boss's radio, and Noah had no control over whether it was played or not.

The man singing on the radio at the moment also did a bit of yodeling. It made Noah think of Faith Stutzman and how she'd given up her entertaining career and moved back home. He wondered if she had enjoyed the pie he'd given her and what she thought about the verse of scripture he'd attached. Had it spoken to her heart, the way God's Word was supposed to do? He surely hoped so, for Faith seemed to be in need of something, and Noah couldn't think of anything more nourishing to the soul than the holy Bible.

"Did you bring any of your baked goods in your lunch today?"

Noah turned his head at the sound of his boss's voice. He hadn't realized Hank had moved over to his row of trees. "I made some oatmeal bread last night," Noah said. "Brought you and the wife a loaf of it."

Hank lowered the volume, set his portable radio on the

ground, and hunkered down beside Noah. "You're the best! Sure hope your mama knows how lucky she is to have you still livin' at home."

Noah snickered. "I think she does appreciate my help in the kitchen, but I ain't sure how lucky she is."

"A fellow like you oughta be married and raising babies, like those nine brothers of yours. Between your cooking and baking skills and the concern you show over a weak little tree, I'd say you'd make one fine husband and daddy." Hank nodded toward the struggling pine Noah had been studying before he let his thoughts carry him away.

Noah could feel a flush of heat climb up the back of his neck. He hated how easily he blushed. "I—uh—thanks for the nice words."

Hank clasped Noah's shoulder. "Didn't mean to embarrass you none. I'm glad to have someone as carin' as you working here at Osborns' Christmas Tree Farm."

Noah got to his feet, and Hank did the same. "Thanks. I enjoy workin' here, too."

"You might not say that come fall when things get really busy."

"I made it through last year and lived to tell about it," Noah said with a laugh. The month or so before Christmas was always a hectic time at the tree farm. In early November, trees were cut, netted, and bundled for pickup by various lots. Many people in the area came out to the Osborns' to choose and cut their own tree, as well. Some folks dropped by as early as the first of October to reserve their pine.

Hank's wife, Sandy, ran the gift shop, located in one section of the barn. She took in a lot of items on consignment from the local people, including several who were Amish. Everything from homemade peanut brittle to pinecone-decorated wreaths was sold at the gift store, and Sandy always served her customers a treat before they left the rustic building. Last year Noah had contributed some baked goods for her clientele to try, and his desserts had been well received.

"I need to move on to the next row and see how Fred and Bob are doing," Hank announced. "Want me to leave the radio with you?"

Noah shook his head. "No, thanks. The melody the birds are makin' is all the music I need to hear today."

Hank thumped Noah lightly on the back. "All right then. See you up at the barn at lunchtime."

"Sure thing." Noah moved on down the row of pines to check several more seedlings. As a father would tend his child, he took special care with each struggling tree. Like everything else the good Lord created, these future Christmas trees needed tender, loving care.

As Noah thought about Hank's comment concerning him making a good husband and father, an uninvited image of Faith Stutzman popped into his mind. He could see her look of confusion when he'd given her the pie and then the smile that spread across her face when he'd explained the reason for the gift. Faith's winsome expression and sparkling blue eyes had held him captive that Sunday afternoon, and he'd reminisced about their visit in the kitchen several times since.

"Now why am I thinkin' about her again?" he muttered. No question about it—Faith was a fine-looking woman. From what he remembered of the way she used to be, Faith could be a lot of fun. But Noah was sure there was no hope of her ever being interested in someone like him.

I'm shy; she's outgoing. I'm plain; she's beautiful. I'm twenty-four; she's twenty-eight. I'm firmly committed to the Amish faith, and she's—what exactly is Faith committed to? Noah determined to find that out, as soon as he got to know her better.

five

Noah stood on the front porch of their old farmhouse, leaning against the railing and gazing into the yard. Pap had built this place shortly after he and Mom moved to Webster County, Missouri, from the state of Indiana, soon after they were married. Twenty-three other families had joined them in establishing the first Amish community on the outskirts of the small town of Seymour. Now, nearly two hundred Plain families lived in the area. Some had moved here from other parts of the country, while others came about from marriages and children being born to those who had chosen to stay and make their home in the area.

Noah and his brothers were some of those born and raised in Webster County, and Noah had never traveled any farther than the town of Springfield. He had no desire to see the world, like some Amish did during their running-around years. He loved it here and was content to stay close to home, near those he cared about so deeply.

His brothers Chester, Jonas, and Harvey had moved to northern Missouri with their wives and children, but Lloyd, Lyle, Rube, Henry, William, and Peter had chosen to stay in the area. Each had his own farm, although some had opened businesses to supplement their income.

Noah's thoughts darted ahead to the next day. Church was held every other Sunday, and since tomorrow was a Preaching Sunday, Noah planned to speak with Faith. He wanted to find out if she had enjoyed his Lemon Sponge pie and see what she thought of the verse of scripture he'd attached. He contemplated the idea of taking her another one of his baked goods but decided she might think he was being pushy. From the few minutes they'd spent together, Noah guessed Faith felt uncomfortable, and he figured she probably needed a friend. Maybe he could be her friend, if she would let him.

He gulped in a deep breath of the evening air and flopped into Pap's wooden rocking chair. It smelled as if rain was coming, and with the oppressing heat they'd been having lately, Noah knew the land could surely use a good dousing.

A short time later, a streak of lightning shot across the sky, followed by a thunderous roar that shook the whole house.

"Yep, a summer storm's a-comin' all right," he murmured. "Guess I'd best be gettin' to bed, or I'll be tempted to sit out here and watch it all night." Noah had enjoyed thunderstorms ever since he was a boy. Something fascinated him about the way lightning zigzagged across the sky as the rain pelted the earth. It made Noah realize the awesomeness of God's power. Everything on earth was under the Master's hand, and he never ceased to marvel at the majesty of it all.

Noah rose from his chair just as the rain started to fall. It fell lightly at first but soon began to pummel the ground. He gazed up at the gray sky. "Keep us all safe this night, Lord."

❧

Noah sat up with a start. He'd been dreaming about Pap's pigs when something awakened him.

Strange, he thought as he slipped out of bed. *I don't even like my dad's smelly critters, so it makes no sense I'd be dreamin' about 'em.*

It was still raining. Noah could hear the heavy drops falling on their metal roof and the wind whipping against his upstairs bedroom window, rattling the glass until he feared it might break.

Noah padded across the wooden floor in his bare feet and

lifted the dark shade from the windowpane. He gasped at the sight before him.

Flames of red and orange shot out of the barn in all directions, as billows of smoke drifted toward the sky.

Noah threw on his clothes and dashed down the stairs. He pounded on his parents' bedroom door, shouting, "Pap, get up! The barn's on fire!"

The next couple of hours went by in a blur as Noah, his dad, and several of their neighbors, including Noah's two brothers who lived close by, tried unsuccessfully to save the Hertzlers' barn. It was only a miracle the animals had been rescued, although they had lost one aged sow, and several other pigs seemed to be affected by the smoke.

An English neighbor had phoned the Seymour Fire Department, but they hadn't arrived in time to save the barn.

The storm was over now, and Noah stood in the yard next to his parents, surveying the damage. "I'm so sorry about your barn, Pap," Noah said with a catch in his voice. "If I'd only been awake when it was struck by lightning, maybe we could've caught it in time to keep the whole place from burning."

"It ain't your fault," his father said hoarsely. "Trouble comes to all, and at least no human lives were taken." He shook his head slowly, and Noah couldn't help but notice the dejected look on Pap's face. His wrinkles seemed more pronounced. His shoulders were slumped. Soot covered his hair, skin, and face.

Mom slipped an arm around both her husband's and Noah's waists. "We can have a new barn raised as soon as this mess is cleaned up."

"*Jah,*" Noah agreed, "and I'm sure we'll have plenty of help." The folks in their community always rallied whenever anyone lost a barn or needed major work done on a house.

He was certain it would be no different this time.

"There's nothin' more we can do here," Mom said. "I say we go on back to bed and try to get a few more hours' sleep before we have to get up for Preachin'."

Pap nodded and took hold of Mom's hand. The two of them shuffled off toward the house.

"You comin', son?" Mom called over her shoulder.

"I'll be in after a bit."

Noah heard the back door click shut and knew his folks had entered the house, but he just stood there on the grass, as if glued to the spot. The huge white barn he'd played in as a child was gone. Its remains were nothing more than a pile of charred lumber and a heap of ashes. Soon there would be a new barn in its place. At least that was something to be thankful for.

ಶಿ

Faith awoke on Sunday morning feeling groggy and disoriented. She'd spent most of the night caring for Melinda, who had come down with the flu. The child was running a temperature, complained of a headache, and had vomited several times.

Faith glanced over at her child, now sleeping peacefully on the other side of the bed, which the two of them had shared last night. Melinda usually slept in Susie's room, but Faith didn't want to expose her little sister to the flu, so she'd moved her daughter as soon as she realized the child was sick. Besides, Melinda would be best cared for if she was close to her mother.

Faith slipped out from under the covers, crossed the room, and plucked her lightweight robe off the wall peg where she'd hung it the night before. She would go downstairs, have a bite of breakfast, and come back to bed.

A short time later, Faith found her mother and three sisters in the kitchen, scurrying about to get the table set and break-fast on. The tantalizing aroma of eggs cooking on the stove made her stomach rumble. Until this moment she hadn't realized how hungry she was.

"You're not even dressed," Mama said, scowling at Faith. "And where's Melinda? The two of you are gonna make us late for Preachin' if ya don't get a move on."

"Melinda came down with the flu during the night." Faith reached for the teakettle on the back of the stove. "We'll both be staying home from church today."

"I'm sorry to hear that," Mama said.

"Sorry to hear Melinda's sick or that we won't be going to church?" Faith's voice sounded harsh, even to her own ears, but she didn't like the feeling that her mother disapproved of her staying home from church.

"I don't appreciate the tone you're usin'," Mama said, push-ing her glasses to the bridge of her nose. "I'm sorry to hear Melinda is sick, and I understand why you won't be going to Preachin' today."

Faith felt a sense of guilt stab her conscience. She knew she shouldn't be so quick to condemn her mother. In times past, Mama had seemed so judgmental, and she assumed nothing had changed. Apparently she'd been wrong. Maybe Mama did understand.

"Sorry for snappin'," Faith mumbled. "Guess I'm a mite edgy this morning. Neither Melinda nor I had much sleep last night."

"Am I gonna get sick, too, Mama?" Susie spoke up. She'd been setting the table but stopped what she was doing when Faith began telling about Melinda coming down with the flu.

"I hope not," Faith said. "That's why I moved her from your bedroom into mine."

"If Melinda stays in your room while she's got the bug,

maybe none of us will get it," Mama added from her place at the stove.

"What about Faith?" Esther's pale blue eyes showed her obvious concern. She handed her mother two more eggs. "If Melinda's been sleepin' with her *mamm*, hasn't she already been exposed? Won't she likely get the flu?"

"Guess that all depends on how strong her immune system is," Mama replied. She broke one egg into the pan and reached for another.

"That's right," Grace put in, before she retrieved a jug of milk from the refrigerator and set it on the table.

Faith could hardly believe the way her sisters and mother were discussing her as though she wasn't even in the room. Feeling the need to say something on her own behalf, she spoke up.

"I hardly ever become ill, but have no fear—if I do come down with the bug, I'll be sure to stay put in my bedroom." Faith grabbed a stash of napkins and added them to the silverware Susie had set next to each person's plate.

"If anyone else should get sick, we'll deal with it as it comes," Mama asserted. "Your *daed* and the brothers will soon be expectin' to eat, so right now the only thing we should concern ourselves with is gettin' breakfast on the table."

Faith was glad the discussion was over. All she wanted to do was eat a bite of breakfast, fix a cup of mint tea for Melinda, and head back upstairs to her room.

❧

It was late afternoon when Faith stepped outside to the front porch. She'd spent the day resting and caring for Melinda and was glad the child was feeling somewhat better and had eaten a bowl of soup around noon. Melinda was napping now, so Faith decided to spend a few minutes on the porch swing where she could enjoy the fresh scent still permeating the air after last night's storm. It had been a nasty one, and even if Melinda hadn't kept her up all night, the wind and rain surely would have. When Faith was a child, she'd been afraid of lightning and thunder, but now she merely had a healthy respect for storms. A bolt of lightning could do a lot of damage, and so could the howling winds. Buildings might catch on fire, roofs could be blown off, and flash floods often occurred. None of it was good, and any of the tragedies meant lots of hard work.

When Snowball jumped up beside her, Faith shifted on the swing and stroked the top of the cat's fluffy white head. "You needed to get away from your hungry babies for a while, didn't you?"

Snowball meowed in response, curled into a tight ball, and began to purr.

Faith smiled. Oh, to live the life of a cat, whose only concern was licking its paws, batting at bugs, and chasing down some defenseless bird or mouse now and then. Cats didn't have to answer to anyone. They could pretty much do as they pleased.

She leaned her head against the back of the swing and closed her eyes. It was so peaceful here, where the birds chirped merrily and no one competed with anyone else to get ahead. Nothing like her life on the road had been. She'd had so many demands and pressures that went along with being an entertainer. Days and nights spent in travel, hours of practicing for shows, and the pressure of trying to please an audience had taken their toll on Faith. Still, she would gladly put up with the discomforts in order to be onstage doing what she liked best. *If only my folks could have accepted my humor when I was a teenager. Why was it so wrong to tell jokes and yodel whenever I felt like it?*

Had their disapproval been the reason for Faith's lack of

faith? Or had it come about when she'd married Greg and been mistreated? Faith believed in God—had since she was a girl. But God never seemed real to her. He hadn't answered her prayers, either. Just to be loved and accepted for who she was—was that so much to ask?

Faith's eyes snapped open, and she bolted upright when she heard the unmistakable rumble of horses and buggies pulling into the yard. Her family was home from Preaching. Soon everyone but one brother came streaming up the path toward the house, talking a mile a minute. She noticed John had gone off to the barn, leading the horses.

"You were missed at Preachin' today," Mama said as she stepped onto the porch. "Noah Hertzler asked about you."

Faith's only reply was a slight nod. She didn't care whether she'd been missed or not.

"The Hertzlers' barn burned to the ground last night," her brother Brian said, his dark eyes looking ever so serious. "There's gonna be a barn raisin' later this week."

"Sorry to hear about their misfortune. Was the barn hit by lightning?"

"It would seem so," Papa said as he came up behind Mama. "Sure hope everybody in this house is well by Friday, 'cause all hands will be needed at the Hertzlers' that day."

All hands? Did that mean Faith and Melinda would be expected to help out?

"The little ones will remain at home," Mama said before Faith could voice the question. "Esther can stay here with them, so me, Grace, and Faith will be able to help with the meals that day."

Faith clenched her teeth. So that's how it was to be? Mama had made all the plans, and Faith had no say in any of it. Faith wanted to stand up to her mother and say she was treating her like a child. She could decide for herself if she was going to help at the barn raising and didn't need to be told what to do. She remained silent, however. No point in getting Mama riled up. Faith needed to keep the peace as long as she chose to stay here; it would help ensure her daughter's future. Besides, she did feel bad for the Hertzlers. Nobody should have to lose their barn.

six

By eight o'clock on Friday morning, the air was already hot and sticky. It would be a long, grueling day as the men in their community worked on the Hertzlers' new barn. Faith didn't envy their having to labor under the sweltering sun. At least she and the other women who had come to help serve the men would be able to escape the blistering heat now and then. Their work wouldn't be nearly as difficult, either.

Faith entered the Hertzlers' kitchen, along with her mother and sister Grace. Esther had stayed home to watch Melinda and Susie, as Mama said she should. Eight other Amish women were there as well, including Noah's mother, Ida, and Faith's friend, Barbara Zook. They were scurrying around, getting coffee and lemonade ready to serve the men when they became thirsty or needed a break.

Already the kitchen was warm and stuffy, making Faith long to be anywhere else but there. A dip in a swimming pool would surely be nice. Most of the hotels Faith had stayed at over the last several years had pools or spas, and she often took advantage of both. She'd even taught Melinda to swim, which was a good thing since Faith's folks had a pond out behind their place. At least Faith wouldn't have to worry about her daughter falling into the water and drowning before someone got to her. While not a strong swimmer yet, Melinda could dog-paddle and float on her back.

Faith leaned against the wall and thought about the last time she'd gone swimming with Melinda and Greg. It had been at the hotel pool in Memphis, Tennessee. Greg was in

59

good spirits that Sunday afternoon. He'd won big at the poker table the night before.

When she closed her eyes, Faith could see an image of Greg carrying Melinda on his shoulders. Greg was tall and slender and not particularly well built, but his jet-black hair that curled around his ears and his aqua-colored eyes made Faith think he was the most handsome man she had ever met. The three of them had stayed in the water for over an hour, laughing, splashing, and swimming like a model, loving family would have done.

Only we weren't model, and Greg may have been handsome and charming, but his love was conditional. Faith blinked away the stinging tears threatening to escape her lashes. *Why, God? Why didn't Greg love me the way a man should love his wife? Why couldn't we be a happy family?*

"It's good to see you," Barbara said, jolting Faith away from her memories. "I was hopin' you'd be here today. It'll give us a chance to get reacquainted and catch up on each other's lives."

Faith merely nodded in reply. Truth was, she couldn't allow herself to reestablish what she and Barbara once had or tell her old friend much about her past life. She wouldn't be sticking around long enough to establish any close ties—not even with family members. It was better that way. Much easier to say good-bye when the time came.

"You okay?" Barbara asked with a note of concern. "You look kinda sad."

"I'm fine," Faith fibbed. "Just standing here waitin' to be told what I should do."

Barbara looked a little uncertain, but she handed Faith a pitcher of lemonade and grabbed one for herself. "Let's take these outside to the menfolk. Then we can sit a spell and visit before it's time to start the noon meal."

Faith followed Barbara out the door. They placed their

pitchers on a wooden table beside a huge pot of coffee. As warm as it was today, Faith didn't see how anyone could drink the hot beverage, but then she remembered something her dad used to say. "If I'm warm on the inside when it's hot outside, then my body believes it's cold."

That made absolutely no sense to Faith, and she was pretty sure it was just her dad's excuse to drink more than his share of the muddy-looking brew. She'd never acquired a taste for coffee and planned to keep it that way.

"Let's sit over there," Barbara said, motioning to a couple of wicker chairs set under a shady maple tree.

Faith flopped into one of the seats and began fanning her face with her hands. "Sure is warm out already. I can only imagine how hot and muggy it'll be by the end of the day." She missed the luxury of air conditioning but made no mention of it. No use making an issue over something she couldn't do anything about.

Barbara nodded. "Pity the poor men workin' on that barn."

Faith's gaze drifted across the yard and on out to where the Hertzlers' barn was already taking shape. Rising higher than the family's two-story house, the framing of the new structure looked enormous. Men and older boys, armed with saws, hammers, and planes, were positioned in various sections of the barn. It would be a lot of work, but they'd have it done by the end of the day.

"An English barn is built using all modern equipment, but it doesn't come together in nearly half the time it takes for an Amish barn raising," Faith noted.

"That's 'cause we all pull together when there's a need. I wouldn't be happy livin' anywhere but here among my people."

If Barbara's comment was meant to be a jab at Faith and her wayward ways, she chose to ignore it. "No, I don't suppose you would be."

"Tell me what it's like out there in the world of entertainin'," Barbara said, redirecting their conversation. "Is it all you'd hoped it would be?"

"It's—different—and very exciting. At least it was for me."

"Do ya miss it?"

Faith swallowed hard. How could she tell Barbara how much she missed entertaining, without letting on that she didn't plan to stay in Webster County indefinitely? She moistened her lips with the tip of her tongue. "I miss certain things about it."

"Such as?"

"The response of an appreciative audience to one of my jokes or the joy of yodeling and not having anyone looking down their nose because I'm doin' something different that they think is wrong." Faith hadn't planned to say so much, but the words slipped off her tongue before she could stop them.

"You think that's how your family acted? Did they see your joke tellin' and yodelin' as wrong?"

Faith could hardly believe her friend had forgotten all the times she'd told her about the folks' disapproval. Maybe Barbara had become so caught up in her adult life that she didn't remember much about the days of their youth, when they'd confided in one another and been almost as close as sisters. The truth was, Barbara had even gotten after Faith. Not for her joke-telling and sense of humor, but for her discontent with being Amish.

"Papa used to holler at me for wasting time when I should've been working. He thought my yodeling sounded like a croaking frog, and many times he said I was too silly for my own good." Faith's voice was edged with bitterness, but she didn't care. It was the truth, plain and simple.

"There are others in the area who like to yodel," Barbara reminded her. "It's part of our Swiss-German heritage."

"True, but Papa has never liked it, and it took English

audiences to appreciate my talent."

Barbara's raised eyebrows revealed her apparent surprise. "You really enjoyed bein' English, didn't you?"

Faith couldn't lie, for she was sure the yearning in her heart would show on her face and give away the feelings she'd been trying to keep hidden. She only nodded in reply.

"Then why'd ya come back?"

"I thought it was best for Melinda."

"Your *mamm* tells me you've been widowed for several months."

"That's right. My husband stepped out into traffic and was hit by a car."

Barbara clicked her tongue. "Such a shame it is. I'm real sorry for you, Faith."

"*Danki.*"

"I can't imagine life without my David. We work together in his harness shop, and he's my whole world. Such a *gut* father to our boys, Aaron and Joseph, he is. I don't think I could stand it if somethin' happened to David. It's hard enough to lose a parent or grandparent, but a husband?" Barbara shook her head. "That would be unbearable pain." She glanced over at Faith and gave her a half smile. "Might be a good thing for you and your daughter if ya found another husband. Don't ya think?"

Faith felt her hand go numb from clutching the folds in her dress so tightly. "How old are your sons?" she asked, hoping to steer their conversation in another direction. She didn't want to talk about her dysfunctional marriage to Greg, his untimely death, or the idea of marrying again. Remembering was easy; forgetting was the hard part. Thinking about a relationship with another man was impossible.

"Aaron's four, and Joseph just turned two." Barbara patted her slightly round stomach and grinned. "We're hopin' to have another *boppli* soon. Maybe a girl this time around."

"You're pregnant?" Faith couldn't imagine having two little ones, plus a baby on the way.

Barbara chuckled and gave her belly another tap. "Not yet, but soon, I hope. I love bein' a *mamm*."

Faith enjoyed motherhood, too, and the truth was, she'd hoped to have more children someday. But with the way things were between her and Greg, she had been careful not to let that happen. His unreliability and quick temper were reason enough not to want to bring any more children into their unhappy home, not to mention his drinking and gambling habits. Now that she was widowed and had no plans of remarrying, Faith was certain Melinda would be her only child.

Faith shifted in her chair. *At least Melinda will have her aunt Susie to grow up with. That's almost like having a sister.*

"You'll have to excuse me a minute," Barbara said, standing up. "My David's wavin' at me. He must want somethin' to drink."

Faith stood, too. "Guess I'll go on back to the house and see what needs to be done for the noon meal."

Just before she and Barbara parted ways, Barbara touched Faith's arm and said, "I always enjoyed your joke-tellin'."

"*Danki.*" Faith headed around the back side of the Hertzlers' place, not feeling a whole lot better about things. Barbara's compliment was appreciated, but it didn't replace the approval of Faith's parents. That's what she longed for but was sure she would never have.

She was almost to the porch when she spotted Noah coming out the door. He carried a jug of water and lifted the container when he saw her. "It's gettin' mighty hot out there. Thought some of the men would rather have cold water to quench their thirst."

Faith's cheeks warmed. "Sorry," she mumbled. "Since I

don't drink coffee, and homemade lemonade is too tart for my liking, I should have thought to set some water on the tables."

Noah tromped down the stairs, his black work boots thumping against each wooden step. He stopped when he reached the spot where Faith stood in front of the porch. "I haven't had a chance to talk to you since I gave you that Lemon Sponge pie after Preachin' a few weeks back. I was wonderin' how you liked it."

"It was delicious, Noah. *Danki,*" Faith was quick to say. Maybe she should have sent him a thank-you note. He probably thought she was ungrateful or hadn't cared for the pie.

"Glad you liked it," he said with a friendly grin. "What'd ya think about the verse of scripture attached to the pie pan?"

Faith sucked in her breath, searching for words that wouldn't be an outright lie. "Well, I—laid it aside and kind of forgot to read it." The truth was, she'd thrown the slip of paper away.

Noah's forehead wrinkled. "I'm right sorry to hear that. It was a *gut* verse. One about faith, in fact."

"There's a verse in the Bible about *me?*" Faith giggled and winked at him, hoping he wasn't one who had a dislike for the funny side of life.

A slow smile spread across Noah's face, and he chuckled. "You do still have a sense of humor. You seemed so solemn when we last talked, and I couldn't help but wonder if you'd left your joke-tellin' back in the English world."

She shrugged her shoulders. "What can I say? Once a comedian, always a comedian." So much for being careful to watch her tongue and keep her silliness locked away.

"Do you miss it?" This was the second time today Faith had been asked that question, and she wondered what Noah's reaction to her response would be.

"Sometimes," Faith admitted. "But I'm afraid there's no place for my joke-telling here in Webster County."

"You don't have to set your humor aside just 'cause you're not gettin' paid or standin' in front of a huge audience anymore."

She pulled in her lower lip and released it with a groan. "It's kind of hard to be funny when everyone around you is so serious."

Noah took a seat on the porch step and motioned for Faith to do the same. "We're not all a bunch of sourpusses suckin' on tart grapes, ya know. In case you haven't noticed, there are many among us who like to have fun." He nodded toward two young men who stood beside one of the tables in the yard. They'd been drinking lemonade a few minutes ago but were now running across the grass, grabbing for one another's straw hats and hollering to beat the band.

Faith smiled, realizing Noah had made his point.

"Now back to that verse of scripture attached to the pie I gave you—"

Oh, no. Here it comes. I think I'm about to receive a sermon from this man.

"It was from Hebrews, chapter eleven, verse six."

"And it's about faith, right?"

He nodded. " 'But without faith it is impossible to please him: for he that cometh to God must believe that he is, and that he is a rewarder of them that diligently seek him.' "

She contemplated his words a moment before replying. "Hmm. If it's impossible to please God without having faith, then I must be a terrible disappointment to Him."

Noah tilted his head to one side and squinted at her. "Now why would ya say something like that?"

"Because my faith is weak. In fact, it's almost nonexistent."

"Faith isn't faith 'til it's all you're holdin' on to. Some folks get the idea that faith is makin' God do what we want Him to do." He shook his head. "Not so. Faith is the substance of things not seen."

"Hmm."

"Abraham was the father of faith. When he heard God's voice telling him to leave and go to a new land, he went—not even knowing where he was going."

Faith could relate to that part a little. When she'd first left home to strike out on her own, she didn't have a clue where she was going. She'd ended up waiting tables at a restaurant in Springfield for a time.

"Faith's like a muscle you've gotta develop. It takes time and patience." Noah grinned at her. "Guess that's a little more than you were hopin' to hear, huh?"

She chuckled and nodded. "*Jah*, a bit."

"One more thing."

"What's that?"

"Your name is Faith, so I think that means you've gotta have faith."

"No, it doesn't." She jumped up. "It's been nice chatting with you, Noah, but I have work to do inside the house." She hurried away before he had a chance to reply, glad their discussion was over.

seven

One Saturday morning, a few weeks after the Hertzlers' barn raising, Faith decided to take Melinda into Seymour to check out the Farmer's Market. It would give the two of them some quality time together, which they hadn't had much of since they'd arrived in Webster County. Faith knew her days here were growing short, as she'd had a letter yesterday from Brad Olsen, an agent who wanted to represent her. He asked that she contact him at her earliest convenience, and Faith planned to do so as soon as she felt free to leave.

Faith felt a need to speak to her child in private, encouraging Melinda in the ways of her Amish family and helping her adjust to their new lifestyle. Besides, getting away from the farm for the day would allow Faith to do something fun—something she'd be criticized for if she did it at home. After they had finished browsing the market, Faith had every intention of taking Melinda to one of the local restaurants where they could listen to some foot-stomping country-western music. She'd been to the Hillbilly Café before, when she was a teenager, and had enjoyed the succulent barbecued ribs, as well as the music. While it might do nothing to make Melinda appreciate her new life in Webster County, it would certainly be good for Faith.

Gathering the reins in her hands and waving good-bye to Mama and the rest of the family, Faith guided the horse down the gravel driveway and onto the paved road in front of their farm. It was another hot, sticky day, and the breeze blowing against her face was a welcome relief. There was something to be said for riding in an open buggy on a sultry summer day.

"Too bad it's such a pain in the wintertime," she muttered.

"What's a pain, Mommy?" Melinda questioned.

Faith sucked in her breath. She hadn't realized she'd spoken her thoughts out loud. The last thing she needed was for Melinda to hear negative things about living as an Amish. She'd already complained about the chores she was expected to do.

"It's nothing to worry about, sweetie." Faith reached over and patted her daughter's knee. "Mommy was just thinking out loud."

"What were you thinkin' about?"

"It's not important." Faith smiled at Melinda. "Are you excited about our day together?"

Melinda nodded. "Sure wish Susie coulda come, too."

"Maybe some other time. Today I want to spend time alone with you."

"Will we buy somethin' good to eat at the market?" the child asked.

"We should find plenty of tasty things there, but I think we'll have lunch at one of the local restaurants."

"Can I have a hot dog with lots of ketchup and relish?"

"Sure, honey. You can have anything you want."

Melinda's lower lip protruded. "Grandma Stutzman makes me eat things I don't like. She says I must eat green beans and icky beets whenever they're on the table. How come she's so mean?"

Faith's heart clenched. How could she leave Melinda with her parents if the child felt she was being mistreated? "Vegetables are good for you," she replied.

Melinda shrugged. "I still don't like 'em."

"Maybe someday you will."

They drove in silence for a while, as Faith enjoyed the quiet camaraderie of being with her little girl.

"Mommy, are you ever gonna get married again?" Melinda asked suddenly.

Her daughter's unexpected question took Faith by surprise, and she answered it without even thinking. "No!"

"How come?"

Faith thought before replying this time. She couldn't tell Melinda she was against marriage because she was bitter and angry over the way Greg had treated her. The child loved her father and had no idea what had gone on behind closed doors. She'd kept Greg's abusiveness hidden from their precious child, and she wouldn't take away the pleasant memories Melinda had of her father.

"Mommy, how come?" Melinda repeated.

Faith reached for Melinda's hand and gave it a gentle squeeze. "You're all I need, sweetie."

Melinda seemed satisfied with that answer, for she smiled, leaned against the seat, and closed her eyes. "Wake me when we get there, okay?"

Faith smiled and clucked to the horse to get him moving a bit faster. "I will, darlin'."

&

Faith couldn't believe how many Amish were at the Farmer's Market. When she was a teenager and used to come here, only a few from her community attended. Today several from the nearby Amish community had booths and were selling fresh produce, quilts, and homemade craft items. Others, Faith noticed, were merely there to look, the same as she and Melinda.

Melinda pointed to a booth where an English woman was selling peanut brittle. "That looks yummy. Can we buy some, Mommy?"

"I might get a box, but it will be for later—after we've had our lunch."

"You like peanut brittle?" a deep voice from behind asked.

Faith whirled around. Noah Hertzler stood directly behind her, holding his straw hat in his hands, and smiling in that easygoing way of his.

"Noah. I'm surprised to see you. Are you selling some of your baked goods here today?" Faith asked.

Noah twisted the brim of his hat and shuffled his feet a couple of times. "Naw, I just came to look around."

"We're lookin' around, too," Melinda piped up. "And Mommy's gonna take me to lunch soon."

Noah smiled down at the child. "I was fixin' to do that, as well." He glanced over at Faith. "Would you two care to join me?"

The rhythm of Faith's heartbeat picked up, and she drew in a deep breath, hoping to still the racing. She wasn't sure whether it was Noah's crooked grin or his penetrating dark eyes that made her feel so funny. No Amish man had ever affected her this way, and she found it a bit disconcerting.

Melinda tugged her hand. "Can we, Mommy? Can we eat lunch with Mr. Noah?"

Faith chuckled. "Noah's his first name, sweetie. You should call him Mr. Hertzler."

"Naw. Just call me Noah." He gave Melinda's shoulder a little tap, and she giggled.

"Can we have lunch with *Noah*?"

Faith was surprised to witness the enthusiasm her daughter showed over the possibility of sharing a meal with Noah. Was it because she missed her father so much? Yes, that was probably the reason.

"I had planned to take Melinda to the Hillbilly Café," Faith said, turning to face Noah. "It was my favorite place to eat when I was a teenager."

Noah waggled his dark eyebrows. "That's one of my favorite

places, too. They have some finger-lickin' good spareribs there, not to mention the wonderful coleslaw and baked beans."

Melinda jumped up and down. "Yippee! We're all goin' to the Hillbilly Café!"

⋅ ⋅

Sitting across the table from Faith and her daughter, Noah felt like the luckiest man in the world. Not only was he eating some great-tasting vittles, but he was in the company of two beautiful ladies. At least Faith was beautiful. He guessed it would be more fitting to say that Melinda was about as cute as a newborn kitten.

He grinned at the child, who had a splotch of ketchup smeared on her chin. "Did ya get enough to eat, Melinda?"

She bobbed her head up and down. "But I left room in my tummy for ice cream."

Noah chuckled, and Melinda's mother laughed, too. "I think I'll have my ice cream on top of a huge piece of blackberry cobbler," he announced. "How about you, Faith? Do you care for cobbler?"

She smiled at Noah, and it warmed his heart. "Sure. Most anybody raised in these parts has a taste for that delicious dessert." Faith swiped a napkin across her daughter's face. "You look a mess, you know that?"

Melinda scrunched up her nose. "I don't care. It ain't no fun eatin' a hot dog unless you make a mess."

"*Isn't* any fun," Faith corrected.

"Isn't," the child repeated. "Anyway, can I have some ice cream now?"

"Sure, why not?" Noah blurted out before the child's mother had a chance to open her mouth. "That is, if it's okay with your *mamm*," he amended.

Faith nodded. "I guess it would be all right."

A few minutes later, they'd placed an order for one bowl of

strawberry ice cream and two blackberry cobblers topped with vanilla ice cream.

While they waited for their desserts, Noah listened to the blaring country music and watched with interest as Faith tapped her fingers along the edge of the checkered table-cloth, keeping perfect time to the beat.

The woman who was singing on the radio also yodeled, and Noah marveled at her ability to warble her voice in such a pleasant way. "Oh–le–ee—Oh–le–dee–ee—Oh–de–lay–dee—" Faster and faster the song went, until Noah could no longer keep up with the intriguing sounds.

He glanced over at Faith and noticed that she appeared to be a million miles away. Maybe in her mind she was back onstage, telling jokes or yodeling like the woman on the radio.

"You really do miss it, huh?"

"What?"

"Entertainin'."

Melinda, who had been twisting her straw into funny shapes, spoke up. "Mommy don't tell jokes no more. She gave that up when we moved here to become Amish."

The waitress showed up with their desserts just then, and the conversation was put on hold.

When Noah finished his cobbler, he leaned his elbows on the table and studied Faith. She seemed so somber. It was hard to believe she had ever been a comedian. Didn't the woman realize she could still tell jokes and have fun, even though she was no longer an entertainer?

She looked at him and frowned. "You're staring at me, and it makes me nervous."

He felt his face grow warm. "Sorry. Didn't mean to stare."

"I'll bet you were lookin' at her 'cause she's so pretty."

Melinda's candid statement must have taken Faith by sur-prise, just as it did Noah, for her mouth fell open and her blue eyes were wide. "Really, Melinda—you shouldn't try to put words in Noah's mouth."

"She doesn't have to," he said. "Your daughter's correct. You're a right beautiful woman."

Now it was Faith's turn to blush. "I—uh—don't feel so pretty now that I'm back to wearing such plain clothes." She gestured to her dark green cotton dress, with a matching cape and black apron.

"Beauty isn't about makeup or fancy clothes," Noah was quick to say. "My *mamm* has always said that real beauty comes from in here." He thumped his chest.

Faith sat there silently for several seconds, and then she abruptly changed the subject. "Did you hear about the restaurant that just opened on the moon?"

"No, can't say as I have," Noah said, playing along.

"Well, they have good food, but there's absolutely no atmosphere."

Noah chuckled, and Faith grinned at him. "See, I do still have some humor left in me."

He nodded. "I'm right glad."

"Tell us another joke, Mommy," Melinda begged.

Faith shook her head. "Not now." She looked at Noah. "Why don't you share something about yourself?"

He plunked his elbows on the table and rested his hands under his chin. "What would ya like to know?"

"Do you farm with your dad, or have you found some other kind of work to keep you busy?"

"Actually Pap don't farm much anymore. He's been raisin' hogs for the last nine years." Noah rubbed his hands briskly together. "I work at a nearby Christmas tree farm, and I truly love what I do there."

Melinda's eyes lit up. "A Christmas tree farm? Does Santa Claus live there?"

He chuckled. "No, but it's sure a great place to visit. In fact, I think you'd enjoy seein' all the pine trees that are grown especially for English people at Christmastime."

Melinda licked the last bit of strawberry ice cream off her spoon and turned to face her mother. "Could we go to Noah's work and see the Christmas trees?"

"Well, I—"

"That's a great idea," Noah cut in. "I'll talk to my boss next week and see what we can arrange." He smiled at Faith. "That is, if you're in agreement with the suggestion."

She deliberated a few seconds and finally nodded. "Sure, that sounds like fun."

"Okay. I'll let ya know as soon as I get it set up." Noah leaned back in his seat, feeling happy and satisfied. He had not only eaten a good meal today, but he would be seeing Faith and her daughter again. That thought pleased him to no end.

ﾞ

All the way home, Faith kept thinking about Noah and how at ease he had seemed with her and Melinda. He wasn't the same shy boy she'd known when they were growing up. Back then he barely said more than two words, and he surely never looked at her the way he had today. Noah made her feel uncomfortable when he'd talked about faith and trusting in God, but when he spoke of other things, she felt relaxed in his presence. In fact, Noah's gentle way had settled over her like a soft, fuzzy blanket.

Faith shook the reins, and the horse began to trot. *Makes me wonder why the man's never married. It seems like he'd make a mighty good father.* In the years she and Greg had been married, he had never looked at her, or even Melinda, with the tenderness she'd seen in Noah's eyes today. Was it merely an act, or did Noah Hertzler have the heart of a kind, considerate man?

eight

A few days later, Noah arrived home from work and found Faith's mother sitting at the kitchen table, visiting with his mom over a glass of iced tea. She looked up and smiled when Noah entered the room.

"It's *gut* to see you, Wilma. What brings you out our way on this hot afternoon?"

"Just came by for a little chitchat with your *mamm*. Needed to discuss a few things with someone, that's all."

Noah tried to act casual, but he was curious to know what kind of things Faith's mother needed to talk about. Did it concern Faith? Did she know Noah had invited Faith and Melinda to visit his place of work? Had she come to ask his mother to discourage him from seeing Faith?

He went to the cupboard, took out a glass, and got himself a drink of cool water at the sink. "Want me to make myself scarce so you womenfolk can talk?"

"Naw, I don't have nothin' to say that you can't hear," Wilma responded.

Noah shrugged and gulped down the glass of water.

"So, Noah, how are you these days?"

He wiped his mouth with the back of his hand. "I'm *gut*. And you?"

Wilma blinked a couple of times and shrugged her shoulders. "Fair to middlin'."

"Glad to hear it. How's the rest of the family?"

"Most are doin' okay. Grace is still workin' at Graber's General Store, and Esther's helpin' out at the Lapps' place now.

76

Sally Lapp had triplets awhile back, ya know."

"Guess she'd been needin' a *Maad* then, what with this bein' her first delivery and all," Noah's mother interjected.

Noah moved across the room in the direction of the refrigerator. "Want me to start supper, Mom?"

"*Jah*, sure, if ya want to."

He grinned at his mother. "You know me—always like to cook. I'll keep it simple and cool, since it's hot already in the kitchen."

"That's a *gut* boy you've got there, Ida," Wilma said. "Not like my Faith, who doesn't seem to know what she's wantin' outta life. I left her home to fix supper and do a few other chores, but no tellin' what I'll find when I get back home."

Noah's ears perked up at the mention of Faith's name, but he forced himself to concentrate on supper preparations so it wouldn't appear as if he was eavesdropping. He grabbed a plate of sliced ham, along with a bag of chopped-up lettuce and tomatoes, then shut the refrigerator door. Noah hauled everything over to the counter, took out a wooden bowl from the cupboard, and proceeded to cut the ham into small chunks. Soon he would have a salad going, and the rest of the ham would be used for sandwiches.

"Seems to me Faith knows what she wants," Mom said to Wilma. "She gave up her worldly ways and brought her daughter home, ain't it so?"

Wilma didn't say anything for several seconds, and Noah made his way back to the refrigerator for more salad ingredients. He'd picked up a few radishes and some green onions when Wilma spoke again.

"I don't think Faith's plannin' to stick around. I'm pretty sure she only came home to drop off Melinda so she could be on her own in the English world once more."

Noah heard the sharp intake of his mother's breath, and he

nearly dropped the bottle of salad dressing he'd grabbed out of the refrigerator. Faith not staying? Could the woman really leave her daughter with family she barely knew and head back on the road to pursue her career?

"Ach, my!" Mom exclaimed. "No *mamm* could leave her little one like that. Not for love nor money."

"Maybe not most, but Faith's always had a mind of her own." Wilma's tone sounded resentful, and when he took a sideways glance, Noah saw her mouth quiver.

"What makes you think she's aimin' to leave? Have ya come right out and asked if that's what she's plannin' to do?" Noah had voiced the questions before he even had time to think.

Both women turned to look at him, and he felt his face heat up.

"I—uh—couldn't help overhearing what you said." Noah scrubbed his hand across his chin, realizing he'd forgotten to shave that morning. "Sorry for buttin' into a conversation that was none of my business."

"It makes no never mind," Wilma said. "To answer one of your questions—I haven't asked her outright, 'cause I'm afraid of what the answer will be."

"But how do you know she has leavin' on her mind?" Noah persisted. He bumped the refrigerator door shut with his knee and headed back across the room.

"I've caught her yodelin' a few times, when she didn't think anyone was around."

"Others in our community yodel," Noah's mother said.

"True, but Faith knows her *daed* don't like it, and besides, she's been actin' real strange since she and Melinda first arrived at our place."

"Strange? In what way?" he asked.

"She won't make a decision to be baptized and join the church. Not even after talkin' with the bishop. And she don't

seem the least bit interested in readin' her Bible, neither."
Wilma drew in a deep breath and released it with a groan. "A
smart *mamm* knows when her daughter's tryin' to pull the wool
over her eyes."

Noah felt as if his heart had sunk clear to his toes. He was
just beginning to get acquainted with Faith and had hoped
she'd be sticking around. If for no other reason, she needed to
stay for her daughter's sake. Didn't she realize the child needed
her mother close by?

"Like as not, I'm sure Faith will tell ya what's on her mind
when the time's right," Mom said as she reached for her glass
of iced tea.

Wilma moaned. "Most likely she'll sneak off without sayin'
anything a'tall. Probably will leave us a note on the kitchen
table, same as she did when she ran away from home ten
years ago."

"I'm so sorry, Wilma," Noah's mother said softly. "I'll
surely be prayin' for Faith now that I know your concerns."

Noah glanced over his shoulder at Faith's mother. She was
shaking her head and frowning. "I pray daily for Faith and
her spiritual well-being," the woman said with a catch in her
voice. "I have ever since she up and left home. Fact is, I'd do
almost anything to keep her from leavin' again."

"*Jah*, I would, too, if one of my boys had ever run off."
Noah's mother laid a hand on Wilma's arm. "Never give up
prayin'. God knows what's best for Faith, and might could be
He's got other plans for her that don't include runnin' with the
world. Maybe she don't figure on leavin' a'tall. There's always
the chance you've misread her intentions."

"I hope so, Ida. *Jah*, I surely do."

At that moment, Noah made a decision. He'd wanted to
befriend Faith Stutzman, and now he knew why. If she truly
was thinking of leaving and had no plans to join the church,

he'd do all he could to help her see the need for God as well as her family. Come tomorrow morning, he'd speak to his boss and see about bringing Faith and Melinda by the tree farm on Saturday morning. He'd promised to do so and hadn't yet found the time. By the weekend, Noah hoped he and Faith would be on their way to the beginning of a good friendship. One that might keep the yodeling woman in Webster County.

❧

As Faith stood in front of the propane-operated stove, stirring a pot of chicken broth, she heard a horse and buggy pull into the yard. She figured it was probably someone come to see Papa, who was out in the barn just now. Faith had been left in charge of fixing supper, as well as looking out for Melinda and Susie, while Mom, Grace, and Esther picked peas in the garden, which would soon be added to the steaming kettle of broth. The dumpling dough had already been mixed and was ready to go, and the girls were busy setting the table. As much as Faith disliked cooking, it was preferable to being outside in the hot sun, plucking sticky pea pods off the vine. How Mama, at age fifty-two, could work from sunup to sunset without a complaint was beyond Faith's comprehension.

A knock at the door startled her, and Faith nearly dropped the wooden spoon.

"I'll get it," Melinda offered.

"Thanks, sweetie."

A few seconds later, Faith heard the back door creak open. When she turned her head, she was surprised to see Noah Hertzler standing on the porch, his straw hat held in one hand.

"Look who came to visit, Mommy. It's Mr.—I mean, Noah," Melinda said as she motioned the man into the room.

"If you came to see Papa or one of the brothers, they're out in the barn," Susie piped up. She placed a glass on the table and moved over to where Noah and Melinda stood by the door.

"Actually it's you I'm here to see," Noah said, pointing to Melinda. "You and your *mamm*."

His gaze shifted to Faith, and she gripped the spoon in her hand to keep it from shaking. "What would you be needing to see me and my daughter about?"

Noah took a few steps toward her. "I was on my way home from work and wanted to tell you I arranged with my boss to give you and Melinda a tour of the Christmas tree farm this Saturday. Would ya be able to go then?"

Melinda bounced up and down. "Yes! Yes! The Christmas tree farm! Can we go, Mommy? Can we, please?"

"Well, I—"

"Me, too?" Susie begged. "I've never been to a tree farm before."

Noah looked down at Susie and smiled. "You, too, if it's okay with your *mamm*."

"Oh, I'm sure it will be. I'll go out to the garden and ask her right now." Susie raced out the back door, leaving her half of the table unset.

"How about it, Faith?" Noah asked as he took a glass and set it in place. "Can I come by for you, Melinda, and Susie on Saturday morning around ten o'clock?"

Faith pursed her lips in thought, uncertain as to how to reply. She didn't want to disappoint Melinda, or Susie either. But did she really want to spend several hours in the company of a man who stole her breath away and made her hands feel clammy every time he came near? She'd been through all those giddy feelings with Greg and wasn't about to set herself up for it again. She didn't need a man. She'd had one man once, and what good had he done for her? Sure, Greg had gotten her plenty of shows, but it had been purely for selfish gains, not because he loved her and wanted to see her succeed.

"We could take along a picnic lunch and have us a nice meal at one of the tables under the shady red maple tree in front of Sandy's Gift Shop," Noah said.

"Who's Sandy?" Faith questioned, as she brought her thoughts back to the present.

"Hank's wife. She runs a little store on the Christmas tree farm. Sells everything from peanut brittle to potholders in one half of their barn."

"Sounds like an interesting place."

"It is. I love workin' on the tree farm, and poppin' into the gift store from time to time is an added bonus. I've even donated some baked goods for Sandy to share with her customers." Noah grabbed a handful of napkins out of the wicker basket in the center of the table and began folding each one, then placing them beside the plates.

Is this man for real? Greg was never so helpful. Faith shook her head and mentally scolded herself for comparing Noah to her deceased husband. It was pointless to do so. Especially since she'd be leaving soon, and there was no hope of establishing a relationship with Noah or anyone else.

The back door was thrown wide open, and Susie raced into the room. Her forehead glistened with sweat, and her cheeks were flushed. "Mama says I can go see the tree farm on Saturday," she said, panting.

"Yippee!" Melinda grabbed her aunt's hands, and the two of them jumped up and down like a couple of hopping toads. "We're going to see the Christmas trees! We're going to see the Christmas trees!" the girls chanted in unison.

"Now hold on a minute, you two," Noah said, shaking his head. "Faith hasn't agreed to go yet."

The children stopped their exuberant jumping and looked up at Faith. She lifted one hand in defeat. "Okay. We'll go to the Christmas tree farm."

"Yeah!" Melinda shouted. She grabbed Susie and gave her a hug.

"You had better get busy and fill those water glasses now, *schnell*—quickly!" Faith ordered, even though she was smiling when she spoke.

Noah turned toward the door. "Guess I'd best be gettin' on home. Mom and Pap hired a driver to take them to Springfield today, so there's nobody but me to fix supper."

"Why don't you stay here to eat?" Faith said without even thinking. She hadn't checked with Mama, and she wasn't sure she wanted Noah, the good cook, to sample anything she had made. But the invitation was out, and she couldn't take it back.

Noah pivoted to face her, a smile as wide as the Missouri River spreading across his clean-shaven face. "It's nice of you to offer, and I'd be happy to oblige." With that, Noah plunked his hat on a wall peg, rolled up his shirtsleeves, and sauntered over to the stove. "What can I do to help with supper?"

Faith's mouth dropped open. First Noah helped set the table, and now he was offering to assist her with the meal? She could hardly believe it.

When she'd gathered her wits, Faith pointed to the salad fixings on the cupboard. "Guess you can whip up a green salad, if you've a mind to."

He grinned at her. "It'd be my pleasure."

Faith turned back to the stove. She had a feeling tonight's meal would be better than most.

૨૦

Noah was glad he'd decided to stop by the Stutzmans' on his way home from work. He'd been treated to some fine chicken and dumplings, not to mention good company around the table. Eating with Mom and Pap every night was all right, but Noah had really enjoyed the fellowship of the Stutzmans— from Menno, Faith's dad, right on down to Melinda, the youngest child present. It made him wonder what it might be like if he had a wife and children of his own. Of course, it was nothing but a foolish dream. No woman in her right mind would want a shy man with a big nose who liked to cook. At least that's what Noah's brother Rube had told him many times. Mom said Rube was only kidding, but truth be told, Noah figured his older brother was probably right.

"Noah, would ya care to join me out on the porch for a game of checkers?"

Menno's question pulled Noah from his musings, and he pushed away from the table. "I might take you up on that after a bit, but first I thought I'd help Faith with the dishes."

Faith's dad looked at Noah, then at Faith, then back at Noah. "Are ya daft, boy? Nobody volunteers to do dishes."

Noah glanced at Faith out of the corner of his eye. She was sitting to his left, just one chair away. *They do when it's with somebody as pretty as she is,* he wanted to say. Instead he smiled and said, "I just ate a great supper, so it's only right that I show my appreciation by helpin' out."

"You already helped by fixing the salad and setting the table," Faith reminded him.

He gave an exaggerated shrug. "I help my *mamm* do the dishes most every night."

Faith slid her chair back and stood up. "Okay then. I'll wash, and you dry."

nine

Faith didn't know why she felt so nervous, but the idea that Noah was coming by soon to take them to the Christmas tree farm had her feeling as jittery as a cat with a bad case of fleas. She'd been pacing the kitchen floor for the last ten minutes, periodically going to the window to see if he had arrived.

"It was nice of Noah to invite you out for the day. It'll be good for you and the *kinner* to have some fun."

Faith whirled around at the sound of her mother's voice. She hadn't realized anyone had come into the kitchen. "Yes, I'm sure the girls will enjoy themselves today."

Mama's eyebrows furrowed. "And what about you, daughter? Won't you be havin' a *gut* time, as well? Noah's a nice man, don't ya think?"

"It should be interesting to see how Christmas trees are grown," Faith replied, making no mention of how nice Noah was. No use giving Mama any ideas about her and Noah becoming an item.

Her mother grunted and helped herself to a cup of lemon-mint tea. "It wonders me the way our English neighbors put so much emphasis on bringin' a tree into the house at Christmas, then throwin' all sorts of fancy decorations and bright lights onto the branches. Why not just enjoy the trees outdoors, the way God intended us to?"

Faith didn't bother to answer. She knew Mama had her mind set on things. That's how it had always been whenever Faith showed an interest in the modern world. She helped herself to a glass of cold water at the sink and headed for the back door. "Think I'll wait outside with the girls," she said over her shoulder. "See you when we get back home."

Out on the porch, Faith took a seat in one of the wicker chairs and watched Melinda and Susie as they took turns pushing each other on the old wooden swing hanging from one of the huge maple trees.

"I remember the days when I was that carefree," she murmured, closing her eyes and imagining herself as a child again. Faith and her sisters used to play on the swing whenever they had a free moment. Sometimes, when Barbara came to visit, she and Faith would take turns, just as Melinda and Susie were doing now. Those were carefree days, when Faith was more content with her life. Always joking and playing tricks on her siblings, she had actually enjoyed much of her childhood. It wasn't until she became a teenager that Faith decided she wasn't happy being Amish anymore. It was harder to stick by the rules when she discovered so many things she wanted to see and do—worldly things that weren't accepted by her people. Mama and Papa had seemed more critical of her during that time in her life, too. They said things like, "Why don't ya grow up and start actin' your age?" and "Quit playin' around and get to work."

Faith remembered the time she and Dan Miller had hitchhiked into Springfield and gone to the movies. When she returned home in the evening, she'd gotten into trouble for that little stunt. Papa shouted at her something awful, saying if she were a few years younger she'd have been hauled to the woodshed for a sound *bletching*. He said she was rebellious and irresponsible for taking off without telling them where she was going. When it came out that they'd hitchhiked and gone to a show, Papa blew up and gave Faith double chores for a whole month. He said what she and Dan had done was not only worldly but dangerous. What if some maniac had been the one to give them a ride to or from Springfield? They could have been beaten, robbed, or worse. Faith couldn't believe Dan had spilled the beans. He didn't have to go and blab everything like that.

Mama, who had also been upset, made Faith learn a whole list of scriptures over the next several weeks. No wonder she hardly ever read her Bible after that.

The *clip-clop* of a horse's hooves drew Faith's musings to a halt, and she opened her eyes. Noah Hertzler had arrived. She drew in a deep breath, smoothed the wrinkles in her dark blue cotton dress, and stood up. It was time to leave.

ও

Noah was glad to see Faith waiting on the front porch. He chuckled as the girls surrounded him, both begging to "hurry up and let's go."

Soon he had the *kinner* loaded into the back of his open buggy and Faith settled on the front seat beside him. She didn't say much on their drive to the tree farm, but then it was hard to get a word in edgewise with the girls chattering like magpies in the seat behind them.

Twenty minutes later, Noah pulled into the driveway of the Osborns' tree farm. He stopped in front of the hitching post, got out, and headed around back to help the children out. When they were safely on the ground, he turned to Faith, but she'd already climbed down by herself.

He led the way, taking them into the area where the rows of Scotch and white pines had recently been sheared and shaped.

"Look at all the trees!" Melinda shouted as she ran down the lane. "I wish we could see them decorated for Christmas."

"You can," Noah called. "My boss's wife, Sandy, has some artificial trees in her gift shop. We'll stop in there when we've seen the real trees, and you can take a look-see."

For the next hour, Noah showed Faith and the girls around the farm, explaining the procedure that began in the late winter months and continued up to harvest, shortly before Christmas the following year. From late December until early June, dead trees were cut down, and new ones were planted in their place. From the first of April all the way through summer, the grass around the seedlings had to be kept mowed. The larger trees were sheared and shaped during the summer months, and by fall, certain trees were selected that would be sold to local lots and others farther away.

"By the first of November, we start cuttin' the trees; then they're netted, packed, and ready for pickup on Thanksgiving weekend. The Christmas tree lots are usually open for business on the Friday after Thanksgiving," Noah explained.

"Do all English people buy their trees from the lots?" Susie questioned.

Noah shook his head. "Some come out here and reserve their trees as early as October, rather than going to a lot to pick out a tree." He motioned to a group of nearby pines. "This place is really busy during the month of December, and many folks come back to get a tree year after year. Hank keeps his business operating on weekends until Thanksgiving; then it's open daily for folks to come and get their trees and browse through the gift shop."

"We used to get a Christmas tree when we was English. We'd set it up in our hotel room. Ain't that right, Mommy?" Melinda asked, giving the edge of her mother's apron a tug.

"Yes, that's right. We did always have a tree." Faith tweaked her daughter's nose. "And it's *isn't*, not *ain't*."

"Mommy told me yesterday there won't be a tree in Grandma and Grandpa Stutzmans' house," Melinda continued, making no mention of her mother's grammatical correction. "Grandma said it's against their religion."

Noah glanced at Faith and noticed the wrinkles in her forehead. She was obviously not happy about having to give up her traditional English way of celebrating Christmas, and from the pucker of Melinda's lower lip, the child wasn't either.

"Now that we've seen the trees, we can head on up to the gift shop and take a look at all the *wunderbaar* things Sandy has for sale." He hoped his suggestion would put a better light on things. "After that, we'll eat our picnic lunch."

"Yippee!" the girls chorused.

Faith smiled at Noah. "I think you've made their day."

"I hope you're enjoyin' yourself today, as well."

She nodded. "It's been quite interesting."

The next hour was spent browsing around Sandy's Gift Shop. The girls seemed mesmerized by the artificial trees, decorated with white twinkling lights, red balls, and brightly colored ornaments. Faith appeared more interested in the Osborns' two basset hounds, Amos and Griggs, that kept begging her to throw the rubber ball kept in a basket near the front door.

She likes pets. Noah pondered the thought and smiled to himself.

After visiting with Hank and his wife for a while and sampling some of Sandy's delicious peanut brittle, Noah ushered his guests outside to one of the picnic tables. He opened the wicker basket he'd packed that morning and spread the contents on the table.

"Oh, Noah! How do you expect us to eat all this food?" Faith exclaimed as he placed a plate of fried chicken in front of her.

"Just eat what ya can." He added a jar of homemade pickles, a dish of coleslaw, a loaf of brown bread, and some baked beans to the meal.

They paused for silent prayer and dug right in. Melinda and Susie ate two drumsticks apiece, and Faith devoured a thigh, plus a large hunk of white meat. Noah was glad to see her eating so well. She was far too skinny to his way of thinking. He was also pleased to see how much Faith had relaxed. Either she was feeling more comfortable in his presence or her playtime with Hank's hounds had done the trick. Noah figured he'd made some headway in befriending Faith today. Now if he could only think of something to say that might give him an indication of whether she was planning to leave her daughter and go back on the road again. He debated about asking her outright but decided that might put a sour note on the day. Besides, what if it wasn't true? Maybe Faith's *mamm* had been wrong about her daughter's desiring to leave.

When the meal was over, Susie looked for wildflowers, while Melinda took her turn at playing with Amos and Griggs. Noah suggested he and Faith sit on a quilt underneath the shady maples, as the afternoon had turned hot and humid.

Faith leaned back on her elbows and stared up at the sky. "Sure is peaceful, isn't it? I can see why you enjoy coming to work here every day."

Noah nodded and smiled. "*Jah*, workin' with the pine trees gives me much satisfaction."

"How come you're not married and raising a family by now?" Faith asked suddenly.

He rubbed his chin, searching for just the right words. "Truth be told, I've never found a woman who was interested in me in that sort of way."

"I find that hard to believe. You're a hard worker—Hank said so when we were inside visiting. You're also good with children."

Noah felt his ears begin to burn, and the heat quickly

spread to his face. He wasn't used to getting compliments like that. At least not from anyone other than his mother.

"I don't think I'm much of a catch," he said. "I've never even been in love, and to my way of thinkin', without love there's no possibility of marriage. At least not for me."

Faith grimaced. "I married Greg, and I'm not sure either one of us was ever really in love."

"No?"

"Infatuation, maybe, but not real love. I think Greg only wanted me because he thought I could make him rich."

"And did you?"

"Not even close. I was doing pretty well for a while, but Greg spent most of our money on alcohol, and he gambled some." She frowned and looked away. "I don't know why I blurted that all out. Didn't plan on it, that's for sure."

He touched her arm gently. "It's not good to keep things like that all bottled up."

She nodded, and tears pooled in her eyes. "Greg had a mean streak and often took out his frustrations on me, but I've never admitted it to anyone 'til now."

Noah's eyebrows lifted in surprise. "You mean he was abusive?"

She nodded. "A few times he hit me, but usually in places where it didn't show."

"I'm awful sorry to hear that. No man should ever strike a woman." Noah's heart went out to Faith. He had had no idea what life had been like for her in the English world. "Why'd ya stay with him?"

"Guess I was afraid. Besides, Greg got me some good shows, and I needed an agent." She squinted her eyes. "It's not easy to find a good agent, you know."

"Why would ya wanna go back to that way of livin' if it was so hard?"

"Who says I want to go back?"

Noah felt like slapping himself. He hadn't meant to say that, and he surely couldn't tell Faith what he'd overheard her mother telling his *mamm*.

"I—uh—kind of got that impression by some of the things you've said about life as an entertainer. You mentioned that you missed it and all."

"I do miss it, but my place is here now."

Why don't I believe her? She says one thing with her mouth, but that faraway look in her eyes tells me something different.

Noah decided to change the subject. "Did ya ever get the chance to read that verse of scripture I attached to the Lemon Sponge pie I gave you awhile back?"

She chewed on her lower lip. "I—uh—think I did."

"What did you think?"

"It was about faith, right?"

He nodded.

"Faith might give some people high expectations when things are messed up in their lives, but to me, it's nothing more than false hope."

Noah couldn't believe his ears. His own faith had grown so much over the last couple of years. He couldn't imagine that anyone who'd been taught to believe in God would think faith wasn't real. "As I told ya the other day at the Hillbilly Café, I believe faith is like a muscle and needs to be exercised in order to become strong."

She shrugged her shoulders. "Maybe so, but I don't have the strength to do much in the way of exercising religious beliefs. Even if I did, I don't feel the need to have faith in order to be happy. In the modern world are many things that bring joy, and none requires having faith in God."

"I'm thinkin' some people in this life get confused about what they want. You know that old saying about the grass bein' greener on the—"

"—other side of the fence," she said, finishing his sentence. "Now can we change the subject?"

Noah felt deflated, but he didn't want to force the issue. "Sure," he said with a shrug. "What do you wanna talk about?"

"Did you hear about the elderly man who moved to a retirement home and hoped to make lots of new friends there?"

He shook his head. "Can't say that I have."

"The man met a lady, and they spent a lot of time together. Soon he realized he was in love with her, so he proposed marriage."

"Sounds kind of romantic."

Noah's comment seemed to surprise Faith, for she squinted her eyes at him. "Yeah, I guess. Now back to my story—the day after the man proposed, he woke up and couldn't remember what the woman's answer was."

"What'd he do?"

"He went to her and said, 'I'm so embarrassed. I proposed to you last night, but I can't remember if you said yes or no.' " Faith tapped her fingers against her chin. " 'Now I remember,' the old woman quipped. 'I said yes, but I couldn't remember who asked me.' "

Noah leaned his head back and roared. So Faith was beginning to use her sense of humor again. "That was a cute story. Have ya got another?"

She leveled him with a most serious look. "Do bats fly at night?"

He grinned at her.

"Okay, here goes." She drew in a deep breath. "You know, I never got used to driving a car when I lived among the English those ten years I was gone. Especially after I discovered what a motorist really is."

"What would that be?"

"A person who after seeing a wreck drives carefully for the next several blocks."

Noah chuckled. Faith could be a lot of fun when she had a mind to. He hoped they would have more opportunities to spend days like this together. Maybe when he took her and the children home, he would ask about seeing her again.

"Tell me how you learned to bake such delicious goodies," Faith said, changing the subject. "I sure ate my share today."

For the next several minutes, Noah talked about his interest in cooking and said that, even though he did plenty of outside chores, his dad and nine brothers thought he was a bit strange because he didn't mind helping out in the kitchen.

Faith snickered. "My family thinks I'm weird because I don't know much about cooking."

"The chicken and dumplings you made the other night were good."

"Maybe so, but that dish is about the only thing I can fix well. Can't bake like you do, that's for sure." Faith took a bite from one of the brownies he'd brought along. "Umm. . .this is delicious."

"Practice makes perfect," he said with a grin. "I didn't always bake well, but I had lots of fun learnin'."

"I think I need a lot more than practice." Faith held up the brownie. "I doubt I could ever make anything as good as this."

"Sure you could. Where's your faith?"

She looked away. "I told you before—my faith has diminished over the years."

Noah reached for her free hand and noticed how small and soft it felt. He wished he could keep holding it forever. "I'm prayin' for you, Faith," he whispered.

❧

On the ride home, the girls' chattering ceased. When Noah turned around, he saw the two of them leaning their heads together, eyes shut and cheeks flushed.

Faith was quiet, too, as she stared at the passing scenery and spoke only whenever Noah posed a question. Was she thinking about the things they had discussed after their picnic lunch? Could she be mulling over the idea of exercising her faith? He hoped so, for it was obvious the woman sitting beside him needed more assurance—or maybe a renewed faith in God. He thought she needed the kind of promise that would fill her life with so much happiness she would have no desire for the things the world had to offer. She'd proven by her joke-telling that she could be joyful and funny, even when not on some stage entertaining.

Thinking about Faith and the girls in the backseat, suddenly Noah was overcome with the need for a wife and children. He'd never missed it much until lately, and he wondered if it had anything to do with Faith's returning home.

Unless God changes her mind, Faith will probably be leaving, he reminded himself. *Even if we could begin a relationship, I might end up gettin' hurt. Besides, I'm sure from her comments that she doesn't believe in or accept the same kinds of spiritual things I do.* Noah knew he could never take a wife who didn't share his love and belief in Jesus. It would be wrong, according to the Bible. *Even though I can't allow myself to become romantically involved with Faith, I'll still try to be her friend.* Noah knew it would not only hurt Wilma if her daughter left again, but there was also Melinda to consider. The child needed a secure home and a mother. If Faith left Melinda with the Stutzmans, the child might grow up in the faith of her people and be better off in the long run, but she would probably feel abandoned. If Faith should decide to leave and take Melinda with her, that would be equally bad—worse, truth be told.

Noah glanced over at Faith. "I enjoyed the day. Thanks for agreeing to come."

She smiled. "I had fun, too. I'm glad you invited us to see where you work."

"Maybe we can get together some other time this summer. I'd like to hire a driver and go to Springfield to see that big sportsmen's store."

Faith's eyes lit up. "You mean the Bass Pro Shops?"

"*Jah,* I've never been there, but I hear it's really somethin' to see."

"It's billed as the World's Greatest Sporting Goods Store, and there's even a wildlife museum."

"You've been there then?"

She nodded. "A few times."

"Sounds like the place to be," Noah said, feeling his enthusiasm rise. "I'd also like to visit Fantastic Caverns, which are just outside Springfield."

She waggled her pale eyebrows. "Noah Hertzler, you're a man full of surprises."

"I'm not sure I get your meanin'."

"You used to be so shy when we were children, and now you seem to have such a zest for life. I feel as if I'm getting to know a whole different side of you."

He reached up under his straw hat and scratched the side of his head. "I guess maybe I have changed some." *Especially since you came back to Webster County. You bring out the best in me, Faith. You just don't know it.*

ten

Over the next couple of weeks, Faith noticed a change in Melinda. She was finally adapting to the Amish ways and seemed to have established a strong bond with her aunt Susie. She got along well with the rest of the family and was more accepting of Grandma Stutzman, as well.

Maybe now was the time for Faith to let everyone know of her intent to leave. She would contact the agency in Memphis as soon as she was sure her parents were agreeable to keeping Melinda in Faith's absence.

The family had just returned from Preaching, and the bishop had cornered her after the service about being baptized and joining the church. Faith knew she couldn't keep procrastinating or pretending to be someone she wasn't. Her family and others were bound to discover her true motives and learn she wasn't serious about establishing a relationship with Christ or with those in her Amish community.

Faith had a feeling Noah Hertzler already suspected, for he'd been coming around a lot lately, quoting scripture verses and questioning her about spiritual things. Whenever she gave her response, he seemed disappointed.

She was attracted to Noah, and that scared her a lot. Spending time with him made Faith feel different from how she'd ever felt in the company of a man. Maybe it was because Noah seemed nothing like other men she'd met during her years of living among the English. He was soft-spoken, kind, and gentle. Could it be an act? Was Noah too good to be true?

Faith had been looking forward to making a trip to Springfield with Noah and Melinda, to see the Bass Pro Shops and Fantastic Caverns. She knew she couldn't give in to her desire to spend more time with him, though. No way could Faith afford to begin a relationship with a fellow who was wholly committed to being Amish, even if he was the nicest man she'd ever met.

Faith glanced out the kitchen window. Melinda and Susie were running back and forth through a puddle of water in their bare feet, giggling and making a lot of noise.

"Soon we'll be having supper, and afterward I'll inform Mama and Papa I'm leaving. It's past time," Faith murmured. "But first, I should probably tell Melinda."

Faith hurried out the back door and toward the frolicking children. She would take her daughter aside, explain everything to her, and then tell the folks. She hoped Melinda would understand she was doing this for her own good. Faith would promise to come visit as often as she could—most likely whenever she was in the area doing a show or during the time she had off. Melinda might not like the arrangement at first, but someday she would realize her mother had only her best interest at heart.

Faith had just approached the girls when she heard a shrill scream from behind. She whirled around but saw nothing out of the ordinary.

"Help! Somebody, help me!"

That sounds like Mama's voice coming from over there. Faith rushed to the cellar steps and peered down. There lay her mother at the bottom, moaning and holding her leg.

Faith rushed down the steps. "Mama, what happened?"

"I was comin' down to get a jar of green beans to have with supper, and I tripped on a stone that must have gotten knocked down here." Mama winced when Faith touched her leg. "I think it's broken."

"I'd better call Papa and tell him we're gonna have to get one of our neighbors to drive you to the hospital," Faith said.

She hated to leave her mother lying on the cold, hard concrete, but she had no other choice. "Hang on, Mama. I'll be right back."

From that point on, the rest of the day went by in a blur. Papa, John, and Brian loaded Mama into Lester Jenkins's van for the trip to the hospital. Mama was kept overnight because of the swelling from the break, which had to go down some before the cast was put on.

Faith knew there was no way she could leave now. Esther and Grace had jobs working outside the home, so they couldn't be counted on to take care of Mama or run the house while her leg was healing. Faith would have to stick around a bit longer, until her mother's cast came off and she could resume her regular chores. It was a good thing she hadn't said anything about leaving yet.

The next day, Mama came home and settled into the downstairs bedroom, which was usually reserved for guests. With her being on crutches for the next several weeks, it wasn't sensible to try to navigate the stairs.

Once their mother was situated, Faith instructed Melinda and Susie to set the table, while she busied herself making supper. She'd no more than taken a package of meat from the refrigerator when she heard a knock at the back door.

"I'll get it!" Melinda hollered. She scurried across the room and flung the door open.

A few seconds later, Noah entered the kitchen, holding a loaf of gingerbread in one hand and his straw hat in the other.

"I heard about your *mamm*'s broken leg, and I thought she might like this." He handed the bread to Faith, and Melinda shut the door.

"That was nice of you. Would you care to join us for supper?"

He shook his head. "I can't stay that long, but a glass of iced tea would sure be nice. It's mighty hot out today."

Faith went to the refrigerator, took out a pitcher of iced tea, and placed it on the counter. She wasn't surprised to see Noah helping the girls set the table. He'd done it several times before, whenever he stopped by their house after work.

She took two glasses from the cupboard, filled them with ice, poured cold tea into each, and handed one to Noah. "Here you go. That should help cool you on the inside at least."

He smiled, and Faith's resolve to leave Webster County almost melted right on the spot. What was it about Noah that made her feel so sappy? Maybe his easygoing spirit and obvious contentment were beginning to rub off on her. Well, she couldn't allow it to happen. As soon as Mama was back on her feet, Faith would be gone. Plain and simple!

❧

Noah took a seat at the table and swigged some of the iced tea. "That sure does hit the spot." He nodded toward the chair across from him. "Why don't you send the *kinner* out to play so's we can visit awhile?"

Faith nodded her consent, and the girls raced for the back door, giggling all the way.

"Must be nice to be young and full of energy, don't ya think?" Noah asked when Faith took the seat across from him.

"I'd give up dessert for a whole week to be able to run, jump, and play the way those two do. Even with their chores, they still find time for fun and games."

"That's the way it should be. Us adults need pleasure and laughter in our lives, too." Noah pulled a slip of paper from the pocket of his pants and held it up.

Faith seemed interested, as she leaned across the table. "What have you got there?"

"A verse of scripture. I read it this mornin' before I left for work, and I thought it was enlightening, so I copied it down."

Faith sat back in her chair with a look of indifference. "Oh, I see."

Noah couldn't understand why she acted so remote whenever he brought up the Bible. It worried him. Her disinterest could mean she would never decide to get baptized and join the church, which probably pointed to the fact that she wasn't happy here and wanted to return to the English way of life.

"Don't you want to know what the verse says?" he prompted her gently.

She shrugged. "I figure you plan to tell me either way."

"It's from Philippians 4:4. 'Rejoice in the Lord alway: and again I say, Rejoice.' "

When she made no comment, Noah added, "The Bible also says in the book of Proverbs, 'A merry heart doeth good like a medicine.' I think everyone needs a bit of God's merry medicine, don't you?"

"I'm a comedian, so it's my job to try to make everyone laugh when I'm onstage."

He shook his head. "I'm not talkin' about entertainin', Faith. I'm referrin' to good, old-fashioned humor that's simply God given."

"I used to get into trouble with my folks for acting silly and playing tricks on my siblings."

Noah lifted his eyebrows. "Actin' silly ain't so bad, but playin' tricks is another matter."

"You're too good for your own good, do you know that, Noah Hertzler?"

He laughed. "I don't think my *daed* would agree. He took me to the woodshed for my fair share of whippings when I was a boy."

Faith clicked her tongue. "I find that hard to believe."

"It's true."

"Well, be that as it may, I think you're a do-gooder."

"Is that a bad thing?"

"I guess not, but it makes me feel guilty for being such a sinner and all." A pained expression crossed her face, and Noah's heart went out to Faith.

He reached across the table and laid his hand on top of hers. "Would it be all right if I pray for your *mamm*?"

"Here? Now?"

"*Jah*, if you wouldn't mind."

"I–I guess it's okay."

He bowed his head, and Faith did the same. "Heavenly Father, please help Wilma's leg to heal just right and help her not to be impatient, but to relax and rest, knowing her oldest daughter is here, takin' *gut* care of her."

When the prayer was over, Noah swallowed down the last of his iced tea, pushed his chair back, and stood. "Guess I'd best be gettin' on home. Mom wasn't feelin' too well this morning, and she'll probably need me to fix supper."

Faith scooted her chair away from the table. "Thanks for stopping by with the gingerbread. I'm sure Mama will appreciate it."

He winked at her. "You be sure to have a hunk, ya hear?"

"I don't think you'd have to twist my arm to get me to try a piece or two."

She followed him to the door, and just before he exited, Noah handed her the scrap of paper with the Bible verse. "I'd like to leave this with you. As a reminder that it's okay to have fun and tell jokes. It would be a sin and a shame not to make use of the talent God gave you."

Faith took the paper and stuck it inside her apron pocket. "It was nice seeing you again, Noah."

"Same here, and be sure to let me know if there's anything

I can do to help out while your *mamm*'s recuperatin'."

"*Danki.*"

Noah bounded down the porch steps, waved to the girls, and climbed into his buggy. He was glad he'd made the stop and looked forward to his next trip over.

❧

Faith watched until Noah drove out of sight. He was a nice man. Just not the right man for her.

She turned to the stove, where she set about preparing a pot of savory stew. She had fixed a fruit salad earlier, and they would have that along with the stew, as well as some rolls that Faith had baked that morning.

As Faith filled the pot with cut-up vegetables, she thought about the verse of scripture Noah had given her. Was her ability to make others laugh really a talent from God? If so, why did it seem to be unappreciated by those closest to her? *I have to get out of here before I go crazy with a desire for something I can't have.*

"I'll go as soon as Mama's back on her feet," she mumbled under her breath.

"Go where?"

Faith whirled around at the sound of Grace's voice. "Nowhere! I—didn't know you were here."

"When I got home from work, I saw Papa heading into the barn, so I went to speak with him," Grace said as she washed up at the kitchen sink. "He told me he brought Mama home from the hospital."

Faith nodded. "She's in the downstairs bedroom, resting."

"Is she in much pain?"

"The doctor gave her some medication, so I think she's as comfortable as she can be."

"That's good to hear." Grace grabbed a clean apron and tied it around her waist. "What can I do to help with supper?"

"Guess maybe you could get out some butter to go with the rolls. There's a fruit salad in the refrigerator, so that'll need to be set out soon, too."

"Glad to help." Grace looked around the room. "Where's the rest of the family?"

"The boys are chorin', the little ones are outside playing, and you already know where Mama and Papa are."

"Esther's not home yet?"

"Nope."

"Would ya mind if I slip into Mama's room and say hello before I help with supper?"

Faith shook her head. "Go ahead. The stew won't be done for another half hour or so anyway."

When Grace left the room, Faith turned back to the stove. Her thoughts, however, returned to Noah.

Faith's skin tingled as she remembered how she'd felt earlier when Noah placed his hand on top of hers. The unexpected feelings his touch had aroused made Faith even more determined to leave Webster County as soon as possible.

eleven

The next several weeks were difficult ones, with Faith working from sunup to sunset. Everything in the garden seemed to come ripe at the same time, and much of it had to be canned. Mama did all she could from a sitting position, the girls helped with the simpler tasks, and a few Amish women had dropped by to offer assistance. Faith gladly accepted everyone's help—even Noah's. He came over at least twice a week on his way home from work and helped Faith fix supper or did some outside chores with her dad and brothers. Then on Saturday, Noah would spend half a day working in the garden, helping with the canning, and doing some baking, as well. It was hard to believe, but he was as much help in the kitchen as he was outdoors.

Faith hated to admit it, but she liked having Noah around. His cheerful disposition as he helped with the chores made her workload seem a bit lighter. Even so, she felt trapped, like a mouse caught between a cat's paws. Would she ever be able to leave here and go back on the road? It was beginning to seem as if the time would never come.

Today was one of those Saturdays Noah had come to help. He was out in the garden right now. He'd volunteered to help pick tomatoes, and Faith had been helping him, but she'd gone into the house to get them both a glass of cold water.

When Faith stepped inside the kitchen, Melinda and Susie, who were making a batch of lemonade, greeted her. She chuckled at the sight. Two little girls were squeezing lemons into a glass pitcher, with more juice running down their arms than was making it into the container.

"Need any help?" Faith asked as she stepped up to the table.

"We can do this," Susie said, a look of determination on her youthful face. "Mama told us how."

"That's right, and we wanted to surprise you and Noah with a glass of cold lemonade," Melinda added.

"Then surprise us you shall." Faith turned on her heel. "You can bring the lemonade out to the back porch when you're finished."

As she stepped outside, Faith smiled. Melinda was adjusting so well. School would be starting in a few weeks, and as soon as she got her daughter settled into that routine and Mama was back on her feet, Faith could finally leave.

❧

Faith didn't know where the summer had gone. But here it was the end of August, and come Monday morning, school would be starting for Melinda and Susie. They still hadn't made it to Springfield with Noah in order to see Fantastic Caverns or the Bass Pro Shops.

"Maybe next spring," Noah had said, but Faith knew otherwise. By spring she'd be long gone.

It's just as well, Faith decided, as she hung a freshly washed towel on the clothesline. *Thanks to Mama's accident and Noah's coming over to help so often, I've already seen him more than I should have. Each time we're together makes me long for. . .*

She grabbed another towel from the wicker basket and gave it a good shake. *I long to be back onstage entertaining—that's what I long for. I won't let anything stand in my way once Mama's up and around and able to resume her chores. I plan to be on a bus heading for my next performance by the end of September.*

❧

On Monday morning, Faith hitched her favorite horse to one of Papa's buggies and drove Melinda and Susie to school. The one-room schoolhouse was only a half mile down the road, but this was Melinda's first time in school, and Faith figured she might need some moral support. At least it made Faith feel better to see her daughter dropped off on her first day.

When she pulled the buggy into the school's gravel parking lot, Faith handed the girls their lunch pails, waved a cheery good-bye, and drove away with a lump lodged in her throat. *My baby is growing up, and soon I'll be saying good-bye for much longer than just the few hours she'll be in school every day.*

The thought of leaving Melinda behind was always painful, but Faith had convinced herself it was for the best. Nothing good could come from Faith's staying in Webster County, and no good could come from hauling her child all over the countryside while they lived out of a suitcase in some stuffy hotel room. Melinda would be better off with her Amish grandparents, where she'd have a set routine and a stable environment.

But she won't have her mother, Faith's conscience reminded her. She pushed the thought aside and concentrated on the road ahead. This morning was much cooler than it had been all summer, and she felt a hint of fall in the air.

Faith breathed deeply, filling her lungs with the fresh, crisp air. Soon the leaves on the maple trees would transform into beautiful colors. Then, as the colder weather and expected winds crept in, the leaves would drop from the trees, making a vibrant carpet on the ground beneath.

Faith had never had much time to enjoy the beauty of nature when she was busy entertaining. Sometimes she was scheduled to do two or more shows a day, and when she wasn't performing, she was practicing or sleeping. The only quality time she'd had with Melinda was on her days off. Greg was responsible for their daughter the rest of the time, and he often hired a babysitter so he could be free to do his own thing.

Faith had no doubt in her mind—it was better for Melinda

to stay in Webster County. For as long as Faith was stuck here, she planned to enjoy every minute spent with her daughter.

~

Noah wasn't glad Wilma Stutzman had broken her leg, but he was grateful for the extra time it had given him with Faith. Not only was he doing something he enjoyed, but the time they spent together was strengthening their friendship. At least he thought so. Faith always acted friendly whenever he came by to help out, and Noah took that as a good sign. She hadn't told him she didn't want to hear any more scriptures or things about God, either.

Maybe it's just wishful thinking, he told himself as he left work that afternoon. *Might could be that the strong feelings I'm havin' for Faith have clouded my thinking. If I only knew for sure what she truly feels. Does Faith care about me in any way other than as a friend? Has her relationship to God grown at all?*

Noah's thoughts came to a halt as he approached the Amish schoolhouse and noticed Faith's horse and buggy pulling into the lot. On impulse, he did the same. It would be nice to say hello and see how Melinda had fared on her first day of school.

Faith apparently hadn't seen him, and she hopped out of the buggy and sprinted toward the school without a glance in his direction. The children were filing out the front door, and Noah sat in his buggy, watching. He would wait and speak to Faith as soon as she had Melinda and Susie in tow.

A few seconds later, Susie came out and climbed into the buggy, but there was no sign of Faith or her daughter.

Maybe she's talking to the teacher. Probably checking to see if Melinda has any homework to do.

Susie turned in her seat and spotted Noah. She waved, and he lifted his hand in response. Then, deciding the little girl might like some company, he hopped down from his buggy, secured the horse to the hitching rail, and ambled over to Faith's carriage.

"Hiya, Noah," Susie said. "You got no *kinner*. How come you're here at school?"

Noah leaned against the side of the buggy and grinned at the Stutzmans' youngest child. She was cute and spunky like her big sister Faith. "Saw your rig and thought I'd drop by and say howdy to Faith."

The skin around the corners of Susie's coffee-colored eyes crinkled, and she leveled him with a knowing look. "You're sweet on my sister, ain't ya?"

The child's pointed question took Noah by surprise. When it came to owning up to his feelings for Faith, he couldn't deny them to himself, but he surely wasn't going to admit such a thing to young Susie. She would most likely blab. If word got out that he was interested in Faith, Noah would not only be the target of teasing by friends, such as Isaac Troyer, but he was sure Faith would find out. If that happened and she didn't return his feelings, Noah wouldn't be able to stand the humiliation.

"Do ya care for Faith or not?" Susie pried.

"Of course I care for her," Noah said, carefully choosing his words. "She's a *gut* friend, and I care about all my friends."

Susie snickered. "That's not what I meant a'tall."

Noah was busy thinking up some kind of a sensible comeback when he caught sight of Faith and Melinda exiting the schoolhouse. As they drew closer, he noticed Faith's furrowed brows and that she looked kind of flustered. He was tempted to rush over to them, but he waited at the buggy until they arrived.

"It's good to see you, Faith," he said.

She pursed her lips and frowned.

"What's the trouble? You look upset."

"Sarah Wengerd. She's the trouble."

"The schoolteacher?"

Faith nodded before she helped Melinda into the buggy. "That woman had the nerve to tell me Melinda seems spoiled and didn't show any interest in learning how to read." Her blue eyes narrowed, and she clamped both hands against her hips. "Can you believe that?"

Noah opened his mouth to respond, but Faith cut him off.

"Sarah insisted Melinda is behind for her age, and she even said I was being defensive when I assured her my daughter is certainly as smart as any child her age." Faith pulled her hands away from her hips and popped the knuckles on her left hand. "I've got half a mind to take Melinda to Seymour and enroll her in public school."

Noah took a step forward, touching Faith lightly on the arm. "I've been around Melinda a lot lately, and I can tell how smart she is. I think she'll catch on quickly to book learnin' and all, if she's encouraged to keep on trying. Would ya like me to start workin' with her? I could drop by on my way home from work a few nights a week."

"It's kind of you to offer, but you've already been coming by our place to help with so many other things. When would you have time to help Melinda with her studies?"

He drew in a deep breath. "How about I come over twice a week, like I've been doing? I'll help you cook or whatever else needs doin'. Then two other days, I'll drop by to work with Melinda. How's that sound?"

"Well, I—"

He took hold of her hand and was glad when she didn't pull it away. "I really would like to do this."

"You've already done so much, and I don't feel right about asking you to do more."

"Please, Mommy? I want Noah to help me." Melinda's tone was pleading.

"Oh, all right," Faith finally conceded. "Noah can help you study."

&

When Noah showed up on Saturday afternoon, he brought along a box of chocolate-chip cookies he'd baked that morning. Melinda was thrilled, and Noah promised she could have some as soon as their lesson was done.

Faith smiled as she watched Noah and her daughter sitting at the table, with Melinda's early reader placed between them. Noah read the words over and over, pointing to each one and asking Melinda to repeat what he'd read.

"I'll be in the next room helping my mother with some mending," Faith said to Noah. "Give a holler if you need me for anything."

He nodded and smiled. "*Jah,* okay. When we're done, I'll let you know. Maybe you'd like to have a few cookies with us?"

"Sounds good. Susie's outside helping Grace dig potatoes. They'd probably like to have some, as well."

"I brought three dozen. Should be enough for everyone."

Faith found her mother sitting in the rocker. Her leg, still encased in a heavy cast, was propped on a wooden footstool.

"Was that Noah I heard come in?" Mama asked, looking up from her needlework.

Faith nodded. "He's here to help Melinda with her reading. He brought along some freshly baked cookies, too. When they're done, we'll have some. Care to join us?"

Mama patted her stomach. "I'd better not. Since I broke my leg and have to sit around so much, I think I've put on a few extra pounds."

Faith took a seat on the couch across from her mother and gathered up the sewing basket sitting on the end table. "I hardly think one or two cookies will make you fat, Mama."

"Maybe not, but with me not gettin' much exercise these

days, everything I eat goes right here." She patted her mid-section again.

Faith shrugged. "Whatever you think best."

For the next hour, Faith and her mother darned socks, patched holes in the men's trousers, and hemmed school dresses for the younger girls. Faith had just finished hemming a new dress for Melinda when Noah emerged from the kitchen. "We're done. Anyone care for some cookies?"

"I do. I need a break from all this sewing." Faith rose from her chair. "Is it all right if we help ourselves to some goat's milk to go along with the cookies?" she asked her mother.

Mama pushed her glasses back in place. "It's fine by me. The goats are producin' in full swing right now, so we've got plenty of milk." She smiled at Noah. "Would ya like to stay for supper?"

"*Danki.* That's right nice of you, but I really should get on home soon. Preachin' will be held at our place tomorrow, and even though several women have been helpin' Mom, I think she still has a few things she wants me to do yet today."

"I hope your *mamm* knows how fortunate she is to have a son like you," Faith's mother said. "My boys are all hard workers when it comes to outside things, but I can't get 'em to do much inside the house."

"My *daed*'s the same way." Noah chuckled. "I like doin' many outside chores, but kitchen duty doesn't make me the least bit nervous."

Faith followed Noah through the kitchen doorway. She still couldn't get over how helpful the man was. For one moment, she let the silliest notion take root in her head. *What would it be like to be married to someone as kind and ready to lend a hand as Noah Hertzler?*

twelve

The day finally came when Mama's cast was removed. Faith wasn't sure who was more relieved—she or Mama. She knew the cumbersome cast must have been heavy, not to mention hot and sweaty with the warm days they'd had in late summer. Only one fly was in the ointment today. Mama's leg, though healed, was now stiff and shriveled up from being stuck inside the cast and not being used for six whole weeks. The doctor told Mama this morning she'd be needing physical therapy. That meant more expense for Faith's folks, and it also doomed Faith to stick around a few more weeks. It wouldn't be right to leave when her mother wasn't yet able to function one hundred percent.

Faith had agreed to go with Mama into Springfield once a week for her therapy treatments, as Papa and the brothers were busy with the beginning of harvest and Grace and Esther were working at their jobs all day. Faith planned to hire one of their English neighbors to drive them, and Mama's first appointment was scheduled for next Monday. Faith was hoping maybe she and her mother could do a bit of shopping while they were in Springfield. At least some window-shopping and maybe going out to lunch at one of those all-you-can-eat restaurants.

❧

On Monday morning, Faith hurried to make the girls their lunches, sent them both off to school with a reminder not to dawdle, and rushed around to clean up the kitchen. She was wiping the table off when she noticed one of Melinda's reading books lying there. She hurried outside with it, calling, "Melinda, come back! You forgot something!"

The children were already halfway up the driveway, but Melinda must have heard, for she spun around and cupped her hands around her mouth. "What'd I forget?"

Faith held up the book. "Come back and get it!"

Seconds later, Melinda had the book and was running down the driveway to catch up to Susie. Faith clicked her tongue and headed back to the house. At least one good thing had happened over the last few weeks. Noah was able to teach Melinda enough to make Sarah Wengerd happy. In fact, the teacher said she was pleased with Melinda's progress and that the child seemed surer of herself now.

Faith knew her daughter liked Noah a lot. She often talked about him, saying she wished he could be her new daddy. Faith tried to dissuade Melinda, reminding her that Noah had his parents to care for, and she and Melinda had Grandpa and Grandma Stutzman to help out. No point getting her daughter's hopes up over something that was never going to happen.

When Faith entered the kitchen a few minutes later, she found her mother limping around the room, putting clean dishes away in the cupboard.

"Why don't you take a seat at the table and have a cup of tea?" Faith suggested. "I'll finish up here, and we'll be ready and waiting when Doris Moore comes to pick us up."

Mama looked a bit perturbed, but she pulled out a chair and sat down. "I'm beginning to wonder if I'll ever get the strength back in my left leg."

"I'm sure with some therapy you'll be as good as new."

"Sure hope so, 'cause I'm getting mighty tired of sittin' around, trying to do things with one leg propped up." Her mother heaved a sigh and poured a cup of tea from the ceramic pot sitting in the center of the table. "Will Noah be comin' over this afternoon when he gets off work?"

Faith shook her head as she slipped a stack of clean plates into one cupboard. "When I saw him at Preaching yesterday, I told him we were going to Springfield this morning for your therapy appointment. Since I didn't know what time we might get home, I suggested he wait until Tuesday to work with Melinda again."

"That man sure does have the patience of Job, don't ya think?" Mama asked. "And I can't get over what a good cook he is, either."

Faith nodded. "You're right—Noah is a good cook, and he does seem to have a lot more patience than most men." Her thoughts went immediately to Greg. He'd been so short-tempered. Especially when it came to her. It seemed as if he expected more from her than she could possibly give. He was always pushing her to do multiple shows and reprimanding her when she wanted to take time off, and he had let his temper loose on Faith more times than she cared to think about. She rubbed her hands along the side of her face, thinking about how hard he'd hit her one night shortly before his death. It had left a black-and-blue mark, but she had hid it under a layer of heavy makeup.

I had to be crazy to stay with that man when he was abusing me, she thought ruefully. In some ways, Faith felt she deserved his wrath. Or maybe she was afraid if she left, she couldn't make it on her own. If Greg had ever hurt Melinda, that would have been it. Faith wouldn't stand for her daughter being mistreated by anyone.

"Susie thinks Noah might be sweet on you," Mama said, pulling Faith out of her disconcerting thoughts. "I was just wonderin' if the feelings might be mutual."

"Susie should mind her own business," Faith muttered

under her breath. She slammed the cupboard door shut with more force than she meant to. Why was everybody trying to pair her up with Noah? Just yesterday, after church was over, Barbara Zook had suggested the same thing. Well, it wasn't going to happen. Faith wouldn't let it. She didn't know if Noah had any feelings for her other than friendship, wasn't sure she could trust him, and knew she'd be leaving soon. There was no point in starting a relationship that had nowhere to go.

Maybe now's the time to tell Mama what I'm planning to do. Give her a little warning, so it won't come as a complete surprise when I'm ready to leave. Faith opened her mouth, but the words stuck in her throat like a glob of peanut butter. Maybe this wasn't the right time. Not with Mama's leg trying to heal.

She popped two knuckles and frowned. *Shouldn't be doing that either, I guess.*

"Faith, what's wrong? You seem kinda agitated," Mama said softly. "Why don't you come over here and have a cup of tea with me while we wait for Doris?"

Faith moved back to the sink, where a stack of clean plates waited on the sideboard to be put away. "I—I'm fine, Mama, and I really do need to get the rest of these dishes put away." *Chicken. You're just afraid to tell her what's troubling you.*

Her mother shrugged. "All right then. Guess we can visit while you work and I sip my tea."

Faith didn't feel much like visiting. Especially if the conversation was going to be centered around her and Noah. Since she didn't feel ready to say what was really on her mind, Faith decided to ask her mother a question. "I was wondering something, Mama."

"What's that?"

"How did you and Papa meet, and how'd you know he was the one you should marry?"

Mama smiled, and her blue eyes took on a faraway look. "Well, your *daed*'s two years older than me, and all through our school days, I had a big crush on him. He never gave me more'n a second glance, though." She took another swallow of tea, and Faith slipped some silverware into a drawer as she waited for her mother to continue.

"Anyways, when I went to my very first singin', I made up my mind I was gonna get your *daed* to notice me, one way or another." Mama smirked and tapped her fingertips against the gray-colored table covering.

"What happened?"

"Menno had taken off his straw hat and laid it on a bale of straw in the Millers' barn. When he wasn't lookin', I snatched the thing up and hid it behind a bunch of old milk cans."

Faith put the last couple of glasses inside the cupboard and came over to the table to take a seat. This conversation was getting mighty interesting, and she wanted to hear the whole story. "Then what?"

"Well, Menno spent the next half hour searchin' for his hat, and in the meantime, my two brothers, Henry and Levi, decided to head for home. Only thing is, they left without me." She snickered. "I think they did it on purpose, 'cause they knew how much I cared for your *daed*."

Faith giggled and poured herself a cup of tea. "I can't believe you would do such a thing, Mama. It doesn't sound like you a'tall."

Her mother slowly shook her head. "I ain't perfect, Faith. Never claimed to be, neither. Besides, I had to do somethin' to get that man to look my way."

"I assume he did, since you're married to him now."

"After I discovered my brothers had run off without me, I conveniently found Menno's hat. When I gave it to him, I just happened to mention that Henry and Levi had gone home and I had no ride."

Faith smiled. "And, of course, Papa volunteered to give you a lift in his buggy."

"He sure did." Mama grinned from ear to ear. "Not only did he drive me home, but when he dropped me off, he let it be known he thought I was pretty cute. Even said he might like to give me a ride in his buggy after the next singin'."

Faith opened her mouth to comment, but the tooting of a car horn closed the subject. "Guess that must be Doris."

"We'd better not keep her waitin'," Mama said. "Wouldn't be good for me to be late to my first therapy appointment."

"No, it sure wouldn't."

&

Noah whistled as he flagged a group of six-foot pine trees with white plastic ribbon. The ones that were six and a half feet would get green and white ribbons. He was selecting these trees to be sold to wholesale Christmas tree lots. Amos and Griggs were at his side, both vying for attention.

"Go play somewhere else, fellows," Noah scolded. "Can't ya see I'm a busy man?"

The hound dogs responded with a loud bark and a couple of wags of their tails; then they bounded away.

A short time later, Hank showed up, offering Noah a bottle of cold water. Noah took it gratefully, as it had turned out to be another warm day.

"Thanks. With the weather bein' so hot, one would never guess it's fall. Sure hope it cools off some before folks start comin' to choose their trees."

"That won't be long," Hank said, as he flopped onto the grass between the row of trees where Noah had been working. Noah followed suit, and the two of them took long drinks from their bottles of water, then leaned back on their elbows.

"I brought you and Sandy one of my Lemon Sponge pies," Noah said. "Dropped it off at the house before I started work."

Hank licked his lips. "Umm. . .sounds good. Maybe we can have a piece after we eat the noon meal."

Whenever Noah made Lemon Sponge pie, he always thought about Faith and the pie he'd given her on that first Sunday after she'd returned home. He'd gotten to know her better since then, and the more time he spent with her, the more he cared about her. He hadn't heard any more from either his mother or Faith's about her leaving Webster County, so he figured maybe she'd given up on the idea of going back on the road. Either that or she'd never planned to go in the first place. Could be that Wilma Stutzman had misread her daughter's intentions. Maybe Noah had, as well, for Faith certainly seemed to have settled into the Amish way of life again—except for not being baptized and joining the church.

For the last few months, Faith had been kept so busy helping out around her place, Noah doubted she'd thought about much else. He saw her staying as an answer to prayer and figured in time she'd make things permanent by joining the church.

"So what's new in your life?" Hank asked then.

"Not so much."

"Are you still helping that little Amish girl with her reading and such?"

Noah nodded and smiled. "Melinda's doin' much better in school, but I've had such a good time helpin' her that I think I'll keep goin' over awhile longer."

Hank shot him a knowing look. "You sure it's not the child's mother you're goin' to see?"

Noah felt his face flame. His boss had hit the nail right on the head. While he had enjoyed helping Melinda with her studies, the real reason he wanted to keep going over to the Stutzmans' place was to see Faith. He took another swig of water and clamored to his feet. "Guess I'd best be gettin' back to work. These trees won't flag themselves."

Hank stood as well. "If you don't want to talk about your love life, it's fine by me." He winked at Noah. "Just be sure I get an invitation to the wedding."

Noah nearly choked on the last bit of water he'd put in his mouth. Was the idea of marriage to Faith even a possibility? He doubted it, but it sure was a nice thought.

❧

The following week, Faith and her mother were invited to attend an all-day quilting bee at Barbara Zook's house. Faith had been trying to avoid her childhood friend as much as possible. Being with Barbara reminded her of the past, not to mention the fact that Barbara seemed determined to convince Faith it was time for her to find another husband.

Mama was insistent on the two of them going to the party, and Faith finally gave in and agreed to attend. She and her mother had been getting along pretty well of late, and she didn't want to do anything to upset the applecart. She'd be telling her folks about her plans to leave Webster County soon, so she wanted the time they had together to be free of disagreements.

On the day of the quilting bee, Faith found herself sitting in the Zooks' living room, surrounded by eight other women. Besides her and Mama, there were Barbara and her mother, Alice; Noah's mom, Ida; and four other women from the community. Two of the women were young and had recently gotten married, and the other two were older ladies who loved to quilt and could do so quite well.

The women enjoyed lots of friendly banter back and forth as they worked with needle and thread, bent over a quilting frame, making hundreds of tiny stitches that would hold the layers of the quilt together.

Faith found herself beginning to relax and have a good time. Before she knew it, she was drawn into the conversation by telling a few jokes.

"Has anyone heard about the English man who met his wife at a travel agency?" Faith asked.

"Can't say as I have," Barbara said in response.

"Well, he was looking for a vacation, and she was the last resort."

To Faith's surprise, all the women laughed, even her own mother, who usually seemed so serious and had never appreciated her jokes before.

"Tell us another one," said Mattie Beyer, one of the younger women.

"Let's see now. . . . An English man approached the gate of an Amish farmhouse one day and was about to enter when he noticed a large dog lying under a bush. The dog seemed to be eyeing him in an unfriendly way, so the man called out to see if anyone was at home." Faith leaned forward slightly, making sure she had the women's full attention. When she realized all eyes were focused on her, she continued the story.

"Now, both the Amish man and his wife came to the front door. 'Come in,' said the woman. 'But what about the dog?' asked the Englisher. 'Will he be apt to bite me?' 'Don't rightly know,' said the Amish man. 'We just got him yesterday, and we're right eager to find out.' "

Everyone howled at this joke, and Faith felt as if she were ten feet tall. Before anyone had a chance to say a word, she launched into another tale.

"The same English man visited another Amish farm, and he was shocked to see yellow bundles of feathers zooming all around the yard. In fact, they were going so fast, he couldn't see them clearly. 'What are those things?' the man asked the Amish farmer who lived there. 'Oh, those are my four-legged chickens. They're pretty quick, don't ya think?' To that, the man replied, 'Yes, but why do you want four-legged chickens?' The Amish man pointed to his wife, who stood on the front porch. 'Me, Nancy, and our two *kinner* all cotton to the drumstick. Now whenever we have fried chicken, there'll be a leg for each of us.' The Englisher pondered the Amish man's words a few minutes; then with a nod of his head, he said, 'So does it taste like normal fried chicken?' 'Don't know yet,' the Amish man answered. 'We haven't been able to catch any.'"

Faith's mother almost doubled over with laughter at the end of that joke, and Faith smiled triumphantly. This was the first time she remembered feeling so accepted or appreciated among those in her community, and having Mama's approval made it even better.

"Have ya got any more jokes to tell?" Barbara asked.

Faith nodded. She was on a roll and might as well enjoy the moment. No telling how long it would last.

"Does anyone know the sure sign that the honeymoon is over for a new bride and groom?"

"No. What is that sure sign?" asked Karen Sepler.

"When the husband no longer smiles gently as he scrapes his burnt toast."

More snickers and chuckles filled the room. This was almost like being onstage for Faith, and she was enjoying it immensely.

"I know one that's true but not so funny," Barbara piped up. All eyes turned to face her, but she looked right at Faith. "It's been proven that having a mate is healthy. Single people die sooner than married folks. So if you're lookin' for a long life, then you'd best get married!"

Faith squinted her eyes at her so-called friend. Wouldn't Barbara ever let up?

"Speakin' of marriage, it won't be long now until we have us a few fall weddings," Noah's mother commented. "In fact, I'm thinkin' maybe my boy Noah might be a candidate for marriage."

Faith's ears perked up. Noah was getting married? He hadn't said anything to her. For that matter, she'd never seen him with any single women. Maybe he was courting someone secretly.

The fun she'd been having with the women drifted away like a leaf on the wind. Faith didn't know why, but a sense of loss suddenly filled her soul. Noah had become a good friend, and if he had a girlfriend, then after he was married, everything between the two of them would change.

It shouldn't matter to me, she reminded herself. *I'll be leaving soon, and what Noah does is his own business. I have no say in it, nor do I wish to have any.* Even as the words popped into Faith's head, she knew they weren't true. She did care, and that's what scared her. She cared too much.

thirteen

It wasn't until the end of October that Faith's mother finished her physical therapy. Only then was she able to get around well enough on her leg so that Faith felt she could handle things on her own.

As she got ready for bed one night, Faith made a decision. In the morning, she would tell Melinda and her folks that she'd be leaving at the end of the week. She'd put it off long enough, and there was no good reason to stay now that Mama was better. All she would need to do was contact the agency in Memphis again and let them know she was available. Until an agent got her a show, she would probably have to launch out on her own, doing one-night stands wherever she could find work. She had done it before, previous to when Greg came into her life, and if necessary, she could do it again.

As Faith glanced at the calendar on the wall, her thoughts went to Noah. November was almost here. He'd probably be getting married soon. After Preaching last week, she'd overheard him telling his friend Isaac that he was interested in someone. Faith wanted to ask him about it that Sunday afternoon but lost her nerve. Besides, it was none of her business. She had her career to think about, and Noah's life was here in Webster County, with his family and friends.

Faith stared out her open bedroom window at the night sky, overflowing with thousands of twinkling stars. She drew in a deep breath, filling her lungs with fresh air. It had rained earlier in the day, and everything smelled so clean. She blinked away sudden tears. *If only my soul was as pure. If only I didn't feel so confused about things.*

ॐ

The following morning, Faith busied herself at the stove, helping Mama fix pancakes and sausage for breakfast, while Melinda and Faith's three sisters set the breakfast table.

Who should I tell first about my plans to leave? Faith had intended to give her daughter some advance notice, but now she wondered if it might not be best to lay out her plans in front of everyone at once. Or maybe she should tell her mother first and get her reaction. If Mama didn't shy from the idea of caring for Melinda in Faith's absence, then she would inform the child.

Faith moved closer to Mama. "There's something I need to tell you," she whispered.

"What's that? I can't hear you, Faith."

"I—uh—was wondering if. . ." She gripped the spatula in her hand. Why was it so difficult to say what was on her mind? "I've made a decision."

Her mother's eyebrows raised. "What sort of decision?"

"I think it would be best if I—"

Faith's words were halted when the back door opened and her father rushed into the kitchen. His face was flushed, and his dark eyes looked as huge as silver dollars.

Mama left the stove and hurried to his side. "Menno, what's wrong?"

He huffed and puffed a few times, as though he was trying to catch his breath. When Mama handed him a glass of water, he shook his head and pushed it away. "*Immer Druwel ergitz*—always trouble somewhere."

"What kind of trouble?" she asked in a tone of concern.

"Old Ben's dead. Found him lyin' on the floor in his stall this mornin'."

Mama gasped, and everyone else stood there like statues.

"I blame myself for this." Papa clasped his hands together. "I've been usin' that horse out in the fields every day this week, and I think I must have worked the poor fellow to death."

Mama touched Papa's arm. "Menno, think about what you're sayin'. You've had Ben for nigh onto twenty-five years. A year ago, you tried to put him out to pasture, but he wasn't content. He liked to work with the other horses and was bound to die sooner or later." She sighed deeply. "At least the horse perished doin' what he liked best."

Papa blinked a couple of times, and Faith wondered if he might be about to cry. Her heart went out to him. "Mama's right," she agreed. "You shouldn't blame yourself for this."

Faith's dad stared past her, as though he hadn't heard anything she said. "The boys and me are in the middle of harvest, so I needed that animal. Jeb and Buck can't do the work of three horses, and I sure can't afford to buy another one just now."

Mama pushed the skillet of hot cakes to the rear of the stove and dropped to a seat at the table. Then she started crying. Grace and Esther went immediately to her side, each of them patting her on the back. Melinda and Susie, obviously uncomfortable with the whole thing, scooted quickly out of the room. Faith, unable to think of anything more to say, stood off to the side with her arms folded.

"If you hadn't had to spend most of our savings on doctor bills 'cause of my leg, we'd have the money to buy a new horse," Mama wailed.

"Guess I could ask some of our church members to help out, but others have needs, too, and I hate to be askin' for more money." Papa took a seat across from Mama and let his head fall forward onto the table.

Mama expelled a few muffled sobs and said something about how sorry she was and how it was her fault for being so careless as to fall down the cellar stairs.

Faith had never seen her folks so distraught, and it worried her that one of them might have a heart attack or something. They sure didn't need another bad thing to happen in this family right now. She moved to the side of the table where her father sat and placed her hand on his trembling shoulder, as she made a painful decision. "I have some money saved up from when I was entertaining. I'll give it to you so you can buy a new horse."

Papa sat up straight and turned in his chair to look at Faith. His dark eyes were wide, and his beard jiggled, as a muscle in his jaw began to quiver. "You'd really be willin' to do that?"

Faith couldn't understand why he was so surprised. Amish family members and friends helped each other all the time. Of course, most offers didn't come from wayward daughters returning home with money they'd made entertaining worldly English folks. Money Faith had been holding onto, so she could start over again when she left Webster County. If she gave her dad the cash, it would mean staying here even longer.

As a lump formed in her throat, she looked at her dad and smiled. This was her chance to prove she wasn't such a bad daughter after all. Maybe even show Papa she cared about the welfare of the family. "I want you to use the money."

He sat there a few more seconds and then finally nodded. "*Jah*, okay. I'm much obliged, Faith, but I plan to pay the money back as soon as I'm able."

"*Der Herr sie gedankt*—thank the Lord!" Mama said with a catch in her voice.

Papa reached out unexpectedly and took hold of Faith's

hand. "I'm right glad you came home, girl."

Faith swallowed hard. She was happy to be helping her folks in their moment of need, but at the same time, she felt a sense of sadness. She had no idea how long it would take for Papa to pay her back. Certainly not until the harvest was over and he'd been paid for the crops he sold. At the rate things were going, she might never again see the bright stage lights or hear the roar of the audience's laughter. If she did finally see her way clear to go, she wondered if she would feel guilty.

❧

Today had been another good Preaching service, but now that it was over and their meal had been eaten, Noah looked forward to speaking with Faith. He'd made another Lemon Sponge pie and planned to present it to her when she joined him under the weeping willow in Jacob Raber's yard, where he'd suggested they meet. He'd attached a note with scripture verses to the pie—from the fifth chapter of Romans, the first and second verses. "Therefore being justified by faith, we have peace with God through our Lord Jesus Christ: by whom also we have access by faith into this grace wherein we stand, and rejoice in hope of the glory of God."

Noah wasn't trying to be pushy, but as Faith's friend, he thought it was his Christian duty to help strengthen her faith. Truth be told, he was beginning to see her as more than a friend, and if there was any chance for them to have a permanent relationship, he had to be sure she was secure in her beliefs.

As he waited for Faith to finish helping the women clear the tables, Noah squeezed his eyes shut and offered up a prayer. *Dear Lord, please help Faith be receptive to the verses of scripture I plan to give her today. . .and receptive to me, as well.*

❧

Faith waved at Noah as she came closer to where he stood under the weeping willow tree on the south side of the Rabers' three-story house. He was smiling from ear to ear and held a pie in his hands. She licked her lips in anticipation. As far as she was concerned, Noah was the best baker in all of Webster County, and she hoped that pie was for her.

"Have a seat," Noah said, motioning toward a quilt spread on the ground.

Faith did as he suggested, and he sat down beside her, placing the pie in Faith's lap. "This is for you."

"Thanks. I surely did need something to cheer me up this morning."

The wrinkles in Noah's forehead showed his obvious concern. "What's wrong? Is your *mamm*'s leg actin' up again?"

Faith shook her head. "It's not Mama this time. One of my dad's workhorses died yesterday morning, and now Papa's faced with buying a new one." She chose not to mention she'd be loaning him the money. No point making it seem as though she were bragging. Faith was well aware of the stand her people took on prideful natures or boasting. *Hochmut*— that's what they called being full of pride.

"That's a shame. I know with this bein' harvesttime and all, everyone needs all the help they can get. And that includes the assistance of their horses and mules." He smiled. "I'm sure once the word gets out, others in the community will help— either with the loan of a horse or money."

"That won't be necessary. It's been taken care of."

"That's *gut*. Glad to hear it."

Faith popped a couple of knuckles, then clasped her hand tightly to keep from doing the rest. If Papa found her habit annoying, Noah might, too. "It sure does seem as if my family has had its share of problems lately. First, Mama falls and breaks her leg; now Papa's horse dies when he needs him the most. It doesn't seem fair, and it worries me that something else might happen."

"The rain falls on the just as it does the unjust," Noah reminded her.

Faith had heard that verse before, but it didn't make it any easier to deal with things when they went wrong. Besides, she wasn't sure she was one of the "just." If Noah or her family had any idea she was planning to return to the English world, they'd see her as a sinner.

"All these problems don't do much to strengthen my faith," she muttered.

Noah motioned to the pie. "I attached another scripture. Maybe that will help."

She groaned inwardly. *Another reminder of the error of my ways. Just what I need this afternoon.* Maybe what she did need was to change the subject.

"Say, I've been meaning to ask you something, Noah."

He tipped his head to one side. "What's that?"

"I overheard your mother talking to Mama awhile back, and I got the impression you had a girlfriend and might be one of those who are planning to be married in November."

Noah's face flamed, and he looked away. Was he too embarrassed to talk about it? "I probably shouldn't have brought it up," she quickly said. "It's none of my business if you've been seeing someone in secret."

"I don't know where my *mamm* got the impression I'm about to be married."

"Then it's not true?"

He shook his head.

"Hmm." Faith toyed with the strings on her prayer *kapp*. "So, you're not seeing anyone at all?"

"Just you."

"Me?" Faith's heart began to hammer. Surely Noah didn't see her in any light other than friendship.

He nodded. "We went to see Hank's Christmas tree farm,

and I've gone over to your place several times to help with Melinda's studies and give you a hand with some chores." He snatched up a blade of grass and bit off the end. "Guess maybe Mom could have assumed we were courtin'."

Faith felt like the breath had been squeezed clean out of her lungs. If Noah's mother thought that, did others, as well? While she felt a sense of unexplained relief to hear Noah wasn't courting anyone, she didn't think it was good if others had linked her and Noah together as a couple. No telling what rumors might soon be flying around.

"It would probably do well if you made sure your mother knows the truth," she said after a long pause. "You know, so she doesn't tell others there's going to be a wedding come November."

Noah chewed on the blade of grass and looked at Faith in a tender way. It made her stomach do little somersaults. "I think I'll let folks draw their own conclusions."

Holding onto the pie, Faith clamored to her feet. "I'd better get going." She wasn't sure what he'd meant by letting others draw their own conclusions, but if Noah wasn't going to let folks know they weren't courting, she certainly was. She'd start with Barbara, who was sitting on the Rabers' porch, blowing bubbles with her two young sons.

"Thanks again for the pie," she called over her shoulder.

Faith went inside the house first and put the pie in the refrigerator. Then she headed for the front porch.

Barbara turned and smiled when Faith stepped outside. "Hey! Wanna join us in some fun?" She lifted a bubble wand in the air.

"Actually I'd like to have a little heart-to-heart talk, if you don't mind."

Barbara scooted over, making room for Faith on the step. "Have a seat, and tell me what's on your mind."

Faith sat down and cleared her throat. "I'd kind of hoped we could talk in private."

"Oh, sure. No problem a'tall." Barbara leaned over and said a few words to her boys in Pennsylvania Dutch.

They nodded eagerly, grabbed their bottle of bubbles, and bounded away.

"I told 'em to go find Susie and Melinda," Barbara said. "Thought maybe the girls would have fun makin' some bubbles, too."

"I know what you said." Faith released an exasperated groan. "I may have been gone ten years, but I still remember our native tongue."

"Sorry. Of course you'd remember."

Barbara's wounded expression let Faith know she'd hurt the woman's feelings. She reached over and gently touched her friend's arm. "Forgive me. I didn't mean to sound so harsh."

"That's okay. All's forgiven." Barbara smiled, and her pudgy cheeks turned slightly pink. "Now, what'd ya want to talk to me about?"

"Me and Noah."

Barbara's smile widened. "Ah, so you two *are* an item. I've been hearin' some rumors to that effect, and—"

Faith held up her hand. "Whoa! Noah and I are not an item."

"You're not?"

She shook her head.

"But Ida Hertzler told my *mamm* that—"

"It's not true. None of it." Faith moaned. "That's what I came to talk to you about. I was hoping you could help squelch any such rumors."

Barbara tapped the toe of her black leather shoe against the step below her. "Sure was hopin' those stories were true."

"What stories have you heard?"

"Just that you two went out to Osborns' Christmas Tree Farm awhile back."

"We took Melinda and Susie along, so it wasn't a date."

"What about all the times Noah's been over to your folks' place? Wasn't he comin' to see you?"

So it was just as Faith had feared. Word had gotten out that Noah had been hanging around the Stutzmans', and people were drawing the wrong conclusion.

"Noah dropped by to help after Mama broke her leg, and he came over to assist Melinda with her studies. That's all there is to it—nothing more."

Barbara pursed her lips. "Sorry to hear that. As I've told you before, I think it'd be good for both you and Melinda if ya found yourself another husband."

"I've been down that road, and it only brought heartaches."

"You mean 'cause your husband was killed?"

"That and other things."

"Such as?"

"There was no joy in my marriage, Barbara." Faith clenched her teeth. "My husband was an alcoholic who liked to gamble and smack me around whenever he wasn't happy. You get the picture?"

Barbara flinched, as if she'd been slapped. "Sorry. I didn't know."

Faith groaned. "No one did. I never want Melinda to know what her father was really like." She blinked back tears on the verge of falling onto her cheeks. "There's nothing good in marriage. Not for me anyway."

Barbara looked stunned. "Don't say that, Faith. Never give up on the idea of marriage or God's will for your life. There's certainly a lot of joy in marriage, if you've got the right man."

Faith grunted. "That's easy for you to say. I'll bet you've never been slapped around by your husband."

"That's true," Barbara admitted. "David has been nothing but kind since we first got married. I've always felt loved and safe with him."

"And with Greg, I always felt about as safe as a mouse trapped between a cat's paws." Faith nearly gagged on the bitterness that rose in her throat.

Barbara's dark eyes looked ever so solemn. "There's joy all around, if you only look for it."

"Maybe for some, but not for me." Faith stood. "Noah and I are only friends, and we won't be finding any joy with one another."

fourteen

For the next couple of weeks, Faith tried to avoid Noah whenever possible. The way he'd looked at her that day under Jacob Raber's willow tree had made her suspicious he might be romantically interested in her. She even thought he'd been about to kiss her, and for one crazy instant, she'd felt a sense of disappointment when he hadn't. Yet she knew it was for the best. She couldn't let Noah think their relationship could go beyond friendship, even though she was beginning to have strong feelings for the man.

Faith was glad she'd had that talk with Barbara. At least now it wouldn't be as likely she'd be thinking a wedding was going to take place between her and Noah. If others saw them together, more rumors would be floating around the community, and Faith didn't need that. But she had promised Melinda and Susie they could go once more to the Christmas tree farm where Noah worked. He wanted to show them how Sandy's Gift Shop looked when it was decorated for the holidays. Faith figured it would probably be their last time together, and since the girls would be there, no one could accuse them of courting.

It was finally November, and the harvesting was done. Papa said he was pleased that Sam, the horse he'd bought with Faith's money, was a hardworking animal and had done his fair share of the pulling as they cut and baled the hay.

Faith was relieved when Papa showed up one afternoon and returned the money he'd borrowed. Now there was nothing standing in the way of her going back to the life of entertaining she'd made for herself in the English world. All that was left to do was inform Melinda and her folks of her plans.

Faith stood on the front porch, staring across the yard, strewn with leaves of various shapes and colors. She did want to resume her career, yet for some reason, the idea of leaving here didn't have as much appeal as it had when she'd first returned home. Faith knew she would miss Melinda something awful, but there was even more compelling her to stay. These last few months, she'd found comfort and security being with family. Life as an entertainer could be lonely. If she were completely honest, she'd have to admit she was going to miss Noah Hertzler, too.

Faith felt as if a war was raging within her. She needed to go yet wanted to stay. *Maybe I'll postpone leaving until after the holidays. A few more weeks won't matter. Besides, I can't go back on my promise to let the girls go to the tree farm with Noah. I'll wait 'til after Christmas to head back on the road.*

ᵟᵉ

The last Saturday of November brought six inches of snow to Webster County. Noah showed up at the Stutzmans' place with his horse and open sleigh that morning. Melinda and Susie seemed as excited about riding in the sleigh as they were about seeing the Christmas trees. Faith was quiet and reserved, as she had been the last few times Noah had seen her. He wondered what could have happened to make her cool off toward him. Until that day he'd given her another Lemon Sponge pie with the verses of scripture, he had thought they'd been drawing closer. Had he been too pushy in trying to help strengthen her faith? Or had it been their discussion about his mother believing them to be a courting couple? Maybe he could get Faith to open up to him today.

Then again, it might be better if he backed off and kept his distance—let the Lord work in Faith's life instead of his trying to meddle and make things happen.

As they headed down the country road toward Hank's place, Noah mentally scolded himself. Mom had told him time and again he had a habit of taking things into his own hands. He hoped he hadn't botched it up where Faith was concerned—with their friendship or with her relationship to Christ. He would try to keep their conversation light and casual today and not even mention anything spiritual.

"Looks like winter's got a mind to come early this year," Noah said, directing his comment to Faith.

"It would appear so," she answered with a slight nod.

"Guess my sleigh will get lots of use over the next few months."

No reply.

"You warm enough? I could see if there's another quilt underneath the seat."

"I'm fine. Thanks."

"You girls doin' okay back there?" Noah called over his shoulder.

"*Jah*. This is fun!" Susie shouted into the wind.

"All we need are some sleigh bells," Melinda added.

Noah chuckled and got the horse moving a bit faster. Soon they pulled into the driveway leading to the tree farm. Amos and Griggs came bounding up to the sleigh, yapping excitedly and wagging their tails.

"The trees look like they're wearin' white gowns," Melinda said, pointing to the stately pines that lined the driveway and were covered with snow.

"You're right about that," Noah agreed.

Hank and his wife stepped outside just as Noah helped Faith and the girls down from the sleigh. The hounds ran around in circles, and the children squealed with delight while they romped in the snow.

"Come inside and get warm," Sandy said, motioning toward her rustic-looking store.

Everyone but the dogs followed, and soon peals of delight were heard as the girls ran up and down the aisles, oohing and ahhing over the brightly decorated Christmas trees. Sandy took hold of Faith's arm and led her toward the side of the store where the crafts were located. Noah figured they'd be having a little woman-to-woman talk, so he moved over to the wood-burning stove where Hank stood. Soon they both had a mug of hot coffee in their hands and were warming themselves by the crackling fire.

Noah glanced around the room. "I'm glad we got here before the rush of customers who will no doubt be comin' by today."

Hank nodded. "By noontime, this place will be swarming with people. Always is, right after Thanksgiving."

"I was in Seymour yesterday after work, and the tree lots there are doin' a booming business, as well."

"That's usually the case," Hank said. He turned away from the fire and looked at Noah, his hazel-colored eyes looking ever so serious. "I know this is probably none of my concern, and if you want me to mind my own business, just say so."

Noah waited silently for his boss to continue.

"I've noticed you've been kind of down in the mouth the last couple of weeks, and I'm wondering if there's something wrong at home."

"Except for Mom's bouts with her diabetes, everything's fine."

Hank took a sip of his coffee. "Your sullen attitude couldn't have anything to do with one pretty little blond, could it?"

Noah knew his face was red, as heat had flooded his ears

and quickly spread to his cheeks. "I'm afraid I might have ruined my friendship with Faith," he muttered.

"How so?"

In hushed tones, Noah explained how he'd been trying to help Faith grow in the Lord and how he had attempted to make her his friend. He said he thought he might have pushed too far and scared Faith off, for she'd been keeping her distance lately, and he was worried.

"Give her some time and a bit of space," Hank said. "If Faith's anything like my Sandy, she don't want anyone tellin' her what to think or do."

Noah snickered. He'd heard Hank's wife speak on her own behalf a time or two and knew Hank was telling the truth. "I came to that conclusion, and I've decided to back off and let God do His work in Faith's life."

Hank tapped Noah on the back. "Smart man."

❧

Faith couldn't believe how many items Sandy had for sale in her store. She saw three times as much as when they'd been there to visit earlier in the year. "I know you make the peanut brittle you sell," she commented, "but who provides all these wonderful quilts, crafts, and collectibles?"

"I buy a few from out of state, but most are made by local people," Sandy explained. "As I'm sure you can guess, the quilts are made by Amish who live in Webster County. English folks—especially tourists—are willing to pay a good price for a bedcovering made by one of the Plain People."

Faith fingered the edge of a beige quilt with a red-and-green dahlia pattern. "They are beautiful, aren't they?"

Sandy nodded. "Do you make anything you'd consider selling here in the store? I'm always looking for new items."

"The only thing I'm good at is telling jokes and yodeling. Mama's the expert quilter in our house."

Sandy's dark eyebrows lifted. "You yodel?"

"I used to be an entertainer, and as part of my comedy routine, I dressed as a hillbilly and would do some yodeling."

A vision of previous times flashed onto the screen of Faith's mind. She saw herself onstage, dressed in a tattered blue skirt and a white peasant blouse. A straw hat, bent out of shape, was perched on top of her head, and black tennis shoes with holes in the toes graced her feet. The audience loved her corny routine, and whenever she yodeled, they always cheered and hollered for more.

"Yodeling sounds like fun. Is it hard to learn how?" Sandy questioned.

Faith shrugged. "Not for me it wasn't. Ever since I was a little girl, I could whistle like the birds and trill my voice. When I went to town one day, I heard a woman yodeling on the radio at the Hillbilly Café. After I got home, I headed straight for my secret place in the barn, where I knew I wasn't likely to be disturbed."

"Did you actually try to yodel right then, with no teacher?"

"I did, and much to my amazement, I didn't sound half bad." Faith giggled. "At least the barn animals seemed to like it."

"I'm surprised your family had no objections to your leaving home and becoming an entertainer."

"Oh, they objected all right. Even before I'd made my decision to leave home, they were always after me for acting silly and sneaking off to listen to country-western music." Faith shook her head. "Papa called my yodeling 'downright stupid,' even though there are others among us who sometimes yodel. He said it sounded like I was gargling or that I had something caught in my throat."

Sandy patted Faith's arm in a motherly fashion. "I guess it's safe to say that with most parents something about their children gets their dander up." She glanced over her shoulder, and Faith did the same. Hank and Noah stood by the stove, obviously engrossed in conversation. "If I ever have the opportunity of becoming a mother, I hope to accept my kids just as they are." She nodded toward her husband. "Hank and I have been married almost ten years, and still the Lord hasn't blessed us with any children."

"Sorry to hear that. Have you thought about adoption?" Faith asked.

Sandy nodded. "We've talked about it, but the process of adoption can take a long time, and it's also expensive."

Faith opened her mouth to say something, but Sandy turned the topic of conversation back to Faith again. "How old were you when you left home, and what did your folks have to say about it?"

"I left the day I turned eighteen, and since I hadn't been baptized or joined the church, they couldn't officially shun me. But when I'd discussed the idea of being an entertainer with my parents at an earlier time, they let it be known they didn't want me to go. Even said if I did, I'd better not come back unless I was willing to give up the English ways and join the church." She groaned. "I took the coward's way out and left a note on the kitchen table, saying I had gone and would never be back."

Sandy looked surprised. She probably thought Faith was horrible for leaving in such a manner. "But you're here now. What happened?"

"Didn't Noah tell you?"

"Not really. He only mentioned you'd been gone a long time and returned home this summer with your daughter. He said your husband was killed by a car."

Faith nodded. "I tried it on my own for six months after Greg's death, but it was hard to find a babysitter for Melinda.

Not only that, but being on the road full-time isn't the best way to raise a child."

"So you decided to give up being an entertainer and move back where you knew both you and Melinda would find love and a good home?"

"Something like that."

"Have you joined the church since you returned?" Sandy questioned.

Faith shook her head. She could hardly tell Hank's wife her plans were to leave Melinda with her grandparents, while she went back to the life of an entertainer. Sandy obviously wanted children, and she'd probably see Faith as an unfit mother—someone who could abandon her child as easily as a frog leaps into a pond. "I—um—haven't felt ready to be baptized and join the church yet."

Sandy motioned to a couple of chairs sitting at one end of the store. "Why don't we take a seat? In another hour or so, this place will be swamped with customers, and I probably won't have the chance to sit down the rest of the day."

Faith followed Sandy across the room, and they seated themselves in the wicker chairs.

"Would you care for a cup of coffee or some hot apple cider?"

"Not just now, thanks."

"Looks like the girls are winding down some," Sandy noted. "I see they're both sitting on the floor underneath one of the decorated trees."

"Those kids are like two peas in a pod," Faith said. "Coming here to Webster County has been good for Melinda."

"And you, Faith? Has returning home been good for you?"

"In some ways, I suppose." Faith didn't want to say more. She might let her plans slip out; then Sandy would tell Hank, who would in turn let Noah know. Sometime between Christmas and New Year's, Faith would be telling her folks she'd be leaving, and she didn't want them finding out before that time.

Sandy drew in a deep breath and released it with a sigh. "Noah has spoken of you and Melinda several times. I think he's grown quite fond of you both."

"Noah's a kind man." Faith stared down at her hands, which were folded in her lap. She resisted the temptation to pop her knuckles. "Noah's good with children and even helped with Melinda's studies when she first started school."

"He mentioned that." Sandy smiled. "I think Noah would make some lucky woman a fine husband. He'd be a good father, too. Don't you think so?"

"I'm sure he would. He's just got to find the right woman."

"Maybe he already has."

Faith was about to ask Sandy what she meant by that comment when Melinda and Susie came bounding up to them.

"Mommy, I'm hungry," Melinda announced.

Faith wagged her finger. "Where are your manners? You had plenty to eat for breakfast, remember?"

"That was a long time ago."

Sandy stood up. "I think I have just the thing that will make your stomach feel happy." She extended her hands to both girls. "Come with me, and we'll go get a big plate of gingerbread cookies and a pitcher of cold apple cider."

The children didn't have to be asked twice, and they skipped off with Sandy to the back of the store.

Faith turned her head toward the wood-burning stove where Noah and Hank still stood. A lock of Noah's dark hair lay across his forehead, and his foot was propped on the hearth. *Noah may not think he's good-looking, but I think he's pretty cute.*

She drew in a shaky breath as the truth hit her squarely in the chest. No man had ever affected Faith the way Noah had, and she was tumbling into a well of emotions that could only spell trouble. She knew she had only one way to stop it, and it would have to be soon.

fifteen

Christmas was the best holiday Faith could ever remember. The entire family had gathered in their dining room for dinner, including Faith's older brothers, James and Philip, along with their wives, Katie and Margaret, and each of their four children. Since both families lived near Jamesport, they'd hired a driver to bring them home.

Everyone had been in good spirits, and the vast array of food was delicious. Even though Faith didn't consider herself much of a baker, she'd made three apple pies using a recipe Noah had given her. They'd turned out fairly well and were consumed before the pumpkin or mincemeat Mama had baked.

But today was the last day of December, and Christmas was only a pleasant memory. In the days ahead, Faith knew she would bask in the recollection of the wonderful time she'd shared with her family—a family she would soon be telling good-bye.

As she stood at her bedroom window, gazing at the snow-covered lawn below, Faith thought about each family member, as well as friends like Noah and Barbara. She knew she would miss each of them after she was gone.

So much for keeping emotional distance from family and friends. Faith grimaced, as her thoughts spiraled further. She'd shared several jokes with the family on Christmas day, and much to her surprise, they'd been well received. No matter how enjoyable the holidays had been, she was sure things would soon go back to the way they had been when she was a teenager. It was only a matter of time before her folks started reprimanding her for being too silly. The time had come for her to leave Webster County, and nothing would stop her this time.

❧

When Faith awoke the following day, her throat felt scratchy. A pounding headache and achy body let her know she wasn't well.

Forcing herself out of bed, she lumbered over to the dresser. The vision that greeted her in the mirror caused her to gasp. Little pink blotches covered her face. She pushed up the sleeves of her flannel nightgown and groaned at the sight. "Oh no," she moaned. "It can't be."

"What can't be?" her sister Grace asked, sticking her head through the open doorway of Faith's room.

Faith motioned Grace into the room. "Come look at me. I'm covered with little bumps. Do you think I could have the chicken pox?"

Grace's dark eyes grew huge as she studied Faith. "Sure looks like it."

Faith turned toward the mirror and stuck out her tongue. It was bright red, and so was the back of her throat. "I thought I had the chicken pox when I was a child."

"Maybe not. You'd better check with Mama."

"Has anyone we know had the pox lately?"

Grace nodded. "Philip's daughter, Sarah Jane, but she seemed well enough to travel, so they brought her here for Christmas anyway." She shrugged. "Probably thought she was no longer contagious or that we'd all had them."

Faith slipped into her robe. "Guess I'd better go downstairs and have a little talk with Mama."

"Want me to send her up? You look kinda peaked, so you might wanna crawl back into bed under the warm covers."

The idea of going back to bed did sound appealing, but Faith had never given into sickness before. All during her marriage to Greg, she'd performed even when she thought she might be coming down with a cold or the flu. Faith had to be really sick before she took to her bed.

With a determined spirit, Faith made her way down the stairs. She found Mama and Esther in the kitchen, scrambling eggs and making coffee. The pungent odor of the strong brew made Faith's stomach lurch, and she dropped into a seat at the table.

"Faith, do you want to make the toast this mornin', or would ya rather be in charge of mixin' the juice?" Mama asked, not aware of Faith's condition.

Faith could only moan in response.

"She isn't feelin' well this mornin', Mama," Grace said, as she stepped up behind Faith and laid a hand on her forehead. "She's sure as anything got herself a fever, and from the looks of her arms and face, I'd say she's contracted a nasty case of the chicken pox."

"Chicken pox?" Esther and Mama said in unison. Mama hurried over to the table. "Let me have a look-see."

Faith lifted her face for her mother's inspection, and Mama's grimace told her all she needed to know. She'd come down with the pox, and that meant she wouldn't be going anywhere for the next couple of weeks. Faith had to wonder if Someone was trying to tell her something. The question was, would she be willing to listen?

"Didn't I have the pox when I was a girl?"

"You were the only one of my *kinner* who didn't get it," Mama said. "I figured you must be immune to the disease."

Faith dropped her head to the table. "I can't believe this is happening to me now."

"What do you mean 'now'?" Grace asked.

"Well, I had planned to. . ." Faith's voice trailed off. She was sick and wouldn't be going anywhere until her health returned, so there was no point revealing her plans just yet.

"Whatever plans you've made, they'll have to wait. You'd best be gettin' on back to bed," Mama instructed. "It's a good thing Susie and Melinda aren't up yet, for unless Melinda's had chicken pox, we'll have to keep the two of you separated for a while."

"She hasn't had them." Faith swallowed against the lump in her throat, as tears threatened to spill over. Not see Melinda for several days? How could she bear it?

If you leave here, you won't see your daughter for longer than that, the voice in her head reminded her.

Faith shuddered and sat up straight. "I think I will go back to my room. Could someone please bring me a cup of tea?"

"One of the girls will be right up," Mama called as Faith exited the room.

A short time later, Faith was snuggled beneath her covers with a cup of mint tea in her hands. If she weren't feeling so sick, it might have been kind of nice to be pampered. Under the circumstances, Faith would sooner be outside chopping wood than stuck here in bed.

❧

Faith spent the next several days in her room, with one of her sisters or Mama waiting on her hand and foot. She heard Melinda crying in the hallway a few times and was tempted to go to her. Not wishing her daughter to get sick, Faith kept her distance, sending her notes and talking to her through the door a few times. It pained Faith to be away from the child, and again she wondered how she was going to leave once she was well enough to travel.

One morning, when the girls were at school and the older sisters had gone off to their jobs, Faith made her way down to the kitchen. She felt better today and decided it might do her some good to be up awhile.

She found her mother sitting at the kitchen table, a cup of tea on her left and an open Bible on her right. Mama looked up when Faith took the seat across from her. "You're up. Does that mean you're feelin' better?"

"Some." Faith helped herself to the pot of tea sitting in the center of the table. Several clean cups were stacked beside it, so she poured some of the warm liquid into one and took a sip.

"Sure was a good Christmas we had this year, don't you think?" Mama asked.

Faith nodded. "It was a lot of fun."

"First time in many years the whole family was together."

Faith's breath caught in her throat. Was Mama going to give her a lecture about how she'd run away from home ten years ago and left a hole in the family? Was the pleasant camaraderie they'd shared here of late about to be shattered?

"You're awful quiet," Mama commented.

"Just thinkin' is all."

"About family?"

Instinctively Faith grasped the fingers on her right hand and popped two knuckles at the same time.

"Wish you wouldn't do that." Mama slowly shook her head. "It's a bad habit, and—"

Faith held up her hands. "I'm not a little girl anymore, and, as you can see, my knuckles aren't big because I've popped them for so many years." As soon as Faith saw her mother's downcast eyes and wrinkled forehead, she wished she could take back her biting words. "Sorry. I didn't mean to be so testy."

Mama reached across the table and touched Faith's hand. "I did get after you a lot when you were a *kinner*, didn't I?"

Faith could only nod, for tears clogged her throat.

"Many times during the years you were gone, I blamed myself for your leavin'."

Faith's eyes widened. "Why, Mama? It wasn't your fault I

wanted something the Amish life couldn't give me."

"I should've been more understanding. Maybe if I'd taken time to enjoy your humor and looked for the good in you, things would have gone better."

Hot tears rolled down Faith's cheeks and stung the pox marks that weren't quite healed. "Oh, Mama, please don't blame yourself for my leaving home. I did it because I felt I needed to, and I'll do it—" Faith stopped before she said anything more. Now was not the time to be telling her plans. She would wait until she was feeling better and Mama wasn't in the mood to blame herself.

Faith took another sip of tea. "Umm. . .this cinnamon apple sure hits the spot."

"Always did enjoy a *gut* cup of tea on a cold winter mornin'." Mama touched her Bible. "Tea warms the stomach, but God's Word warms the soul."

Not knowing how to respond, Faith only nodded.

"Take this verse, for example," her mother continued. "Psalm 46:10 says, 'Be still, and know that I am God.' If that doesn't warm one's soul, don't know what will."

Faith let the words of the Bible verse sink in. *Be still.* She'd been very still these past few days during her bout with the chicken pox. *And know that I am God.*

Faith closed her eyes. *If You're real, God, then would You please reveal Your will to me?*

A knock on the door drew Faith's thoughts aside. Mama rose to her feet. "Must be someone come a-callin' because your *daed* and the boys are out in the barn, and they surely wouldn't be knockin', now would they?"

Faith watched the back door as her mother made her way across the room. When Mama opened it, a gust of cold wind blew in, followed by Noah Hertzler carrying a small wicker basket in one hand.

"Noah, what are you doing here?" Faith questioned. "Shouldn't you be at work?"

He followed Mama over to the table. "Things are kinda slow at the Christmas tree farm right now, so Hank gave me and the others a few days off. This is for you," he said, placing the basket in front of Faith. "I hope it will make you feel better."

She pulled the piece of cloth back and smiled when she saw the frosted brownies nestled inside the basket. "Chocolate— my weakness. Thanks, Noah."

"You're welcome, and it's good to see you up," Noah said, as he pulled out a chair and sat down next to Faith. "The last couple of times I've dropped by, you've been in your room, too sick for visitors."

"Someone in the family has always delivered the goodies you brought me," she said.

Noah chuckled. "Sure glad to hear that. Knowin' those brothers of yours, I wouldn't have been surprised to hear if John and Brian hadn't helped themselves to some of the desserts."

"They did try," Mama cut in. She handed Noah a cup of tea. "Why don't ya take your jacket off and stay awhile?"

Noah set the cup down on the table, slipped his jacket off, and draped it over the back of the chair. "*Danki.* I think I will."

"If you two young people will excuse me, I have some laundry that needs to be done." Mama grabbed a couple of soiled hand towels off the metal rack by the sink and left the room.

Faith had to wonder if her mother had left her alone with Noah on purpose. She'd made a few comments lately about how much she liked Noah and how he'd make a mighty fine husband for some lucky woman. It made Faith think maybe Mama and Barbara might be in cahoots.

"How come you didn't attach a verse of scripture to any of the desserts you've given me lately?" Faith asked Noah.

His face flamed. "I—uh—thought maybe I was gettin' too pushy. Didn't want you to think I was tryin' to cram the Bible down your throat."

Faith smiled. "Guess I probably have needed a bit of encouraging."

Noah reached over and took hold of her hand, and she felt a warm tingle travel all the way up her arm. Not the kind that felt like fireworks, but a comfortable, cozy feeling. "I'm still prayin' for you, Faith," he said quietly.

"I appreciate that, 'cause I think I need all the prayers I can get."

sixteen

By the following week, Faith was feeling much better. The pox marks had dried up, her sore throat and headache were gone, and her energy was nearly back to what it had been before she took sick.

On Saturday morning, after the kitchen chores were done, she decided to have that talk with Mama she'd been putting off far too long. Melinda and Susie had gone to the barn to play. Esther, Grace, and Brian had left for Seymour with Papa about an hour ago. John was over at his girlfriend's house. This was the perfect chance for Faith to speak to her mother alone. When that was out of the way, she would tell Melinda she was planning to leave, which she knew would be the hardest part.

Faith glanced over at her mother, who sat in front of the treadle sewing machine in one corner of the kitchen. "Mama, before you get too involved with your sewing project, I was wonderin' if we could talk awhile."

Mama looked up at Faith and smiled. "Is this just a friendly little chitchat, or have ya got somethin' serious on your mind?"

"Why do you ask?"

"I figure if it's just gonna be easy banter, I'll keep sewing as we talk."

Faith leaned on the cupboard. "I'm afraid it's serious."

Mama slid her chair back and stood up. "Shall we sit at the kitchen table, or would ya rather go into the living room?"

"Let's go in there. We'll be less apt to be disturbed should the girls come inside before we're done talking."

Mama nodded, and Faith followed her into the next room. They both took a seat on the sofa, in front of the fireplace. The heat from the flames licking at the logs did nothing to warm Faith, however. She had goose bumps all over her arms.

Mama must have noticed, for she asked if Faith was cold and suggested she run upstairs to get a sweater.

Faith shook her head and rubbed her hands briskly over her arms. "I'll be okay as soon as I say what's on my mind."

Her mother's forehead wrinkled. "You look so solemn. What's this all about?"

"It's about me and Melinda."

Mama leaned forward, and her glasses slipped down her nose. "What about you?"

"I—uh—plan to go back to my life as an entertainer, and I hope to be on a bus by Monday morning." There, it was out. Faith should have felt better, but she didn't. The sorrowful look on Mama's face was nearly her undoing.

"I knew it was too good to be true, your comin' home and all." Mama squeezed her eyes shut, and when she opened them again, Faith noticed there were tears.

"I never meant to hurt you, Mama. I hope you know that."

"The only thing I know for sure is that my prodigal daughter returned home; only now she's plannin' to leave again." Mama wrapped her arms around her middle, as though she were hugging herself. "No wonder you've put off baptism and joining the church. You've been plannin' this all along, haven't ya?"

Faith nodded solemnly. "I would have told you sooner, but things kept gettin' in the way of my leaving."

Mama stood and moved toward the fireplace. "And Melinda? Will she be going with you?"

Faith jumped up and hurried to her mother's side. "I'd like Melinda to stay here, if that's okay with you and Papa. She needs a good home, where she'll be well cared for and loved. It's not good for a child to be raised by a single parent who lives out of a suitcase and has no place to call home."

Mama turned to face Faith, and she wasn't smiling. The tears that gathered in her eyes moments ago were now rolling down her cheeks. "Melinda can stay if that's your wish. But I'd like you to think long and hard about somethin' before you go."

"What's that?"

"If Melinda needs a good home, where she'll be loved and cared for, then what about her *mamm*? What's she needin' these days?"

Faith nearly choked on the lump in her throat. She was afraid if she said another word, she would break down and sob. She'd made her decision, and this was the best thing for both her and Melinda.

Giving no thought to the cold, Faith dashed out the front door and into the chilly morning air. She headed straight for the barn, because before she lost her nerve, she needed to tell Melinda about her decision.

A few minutes later, a blast of warm air greeted Faith as she entered the barn. Papa had obviously stoked up the stove before he and the others left for Seymour.

Figuring Melinda and Susie were probably on the other side of the barn, Faith headed in that direction. She came to a halt when she heard her daughter's sweet voice singing and—yodeling?

Surprised by the sound, Faith tiptoed across the wooden floor, until she spotted Melinda. The child was kneeling in the hay, with three black-and-white kittens curled in her lap. Susie sat off to one side, holding two other kittens.

"Oddle—lay—oddle—lay—oddle—lay—dee—tee—my mama was an old cowhand, and she taught me how to yodel before I could stand—yo—le—tee—yo—le—tee—hi ho!"

Faith sucked in her breath. She had no idea Melinda could yodel or that she knew the cute little song. Apparently the child had been listening to Faith whenever she practiced, and now she was repeating the same song Faith had sung so many times. Melinda actually had some of the yodeling skills mastered quite well.

When the child finished her song, she looked over at Susie and announced, "When I grow up, I'm gonna be just like my mommy. I'll travel around the country, singin', tellin' jokes, and yodelin'. Oh—lee–dee—tee–tee—oh!"

Faith's heart sank to the bottom of her toes. She'd never dreamed Melinda was entertaining such thoughts. She had been so sure the child was settling in here and would grow up happy and content to be Amish.

The way you were? a little voice reminded her. Faith wanted better things for her daughter than to spend the rest of her life traipsing all over the countryside, hoping to succeed in the world of music or comedy, and seeking after riches and fame.

As though a bolt of lightning had struck her, Faith suddenly realized those were the very things she'd spent ten years of her life trying to accomplish. She wasn't rich. She wasn't famous. Had any of it brought her true happiness? Traveling from town to town, performing at one theater after another was a lonely existence. At least for Faith it had been. Being married to Greg hadn't given Faith the fulfillment she'd been searching for, either. In fact, their tumultuous marriage had furthered her frustrations.

I brought it on myself by marrying an unbeliever. Faith remembered what the Bible said about being unequally yoked with unbelievers. Of course, she hadn't exactly been living the life of a believer during her entertaining years.

She blinked back the tears that were threatening to spill over.

It's just as Mama said—the very thing I've been wanting for Melinda is exactly what I need. How could I have been so blind? I don't need fame or fortune. I've been selfish, always wanting my own way. My truest desire is fellowship with good friends, the love of a caring family, and a close relationship with God.

Faith knew without a shadow of a doubt that if Melinda was ever to settle completely into the Amish way of life, she must see by her mother's example it was a good life. Faith would need to stay in Webster County. It was either that or say good-bye to Melinda and spend the rest of her life wishing she had stayed.

But do I have enough faith in God to live by His rules? Faith knew staying Amish would never work unless she strengthened her faith. She also knew she must rely wholly on the Lord to meet her needs. No amount of money or recognition could fill the void in a person's heart the way Jesus's love did. The verses of scripture Noah had shared over the last few months had told her that much.

It's time to come home, Faith.

She leaned against the wooden beam closest to her and closed her eyes. *Heavenly Father, I need Your help. I know now that I want to remain here with my people, and I want to draw closer to You. Forgive my sins, and please give me wisdom in raising my daughter so she will want to serve You and not seek after the things in this world.*

When Faith opened her eyes, Melinda and Susie were gone. They'd apparently left the barn, seeking out new pleasures found only on a farm. The kittens were with their mother again, just as Faith would be with her child in the days ahead.

Faith found the girls playing in the snow a short ways from the barn. On impulse, she scooped up a handful of the powdery stuff and gave it a toss. It hit the mark and landed squarely on Melinda's arm.

The child squealed with laughter and retaliated. Her aim wasn't as good as Faith's, and the snowball ended up on her mother's foot. Faith laughed and grabbed another clump of snow. For the next half hour, she, Melinda, and Susie frolicked in the snow, laughing, making snow angels, and yodeling. Faith hadn't had this much fun since she was a child.

When it got too cold, Faith suggested they go inside for a cup of hot chocolate and the peanut butter cookies Noah had brought over the other day. The children were quick to agree, and soon they were seated at the kitchen table with a yummy snack in front of them.

Melinda took a bite of cookie and smacked her lips. "Noah sure does bake good, don't ya think?"

"Yes, he does."

"I really like him, don't you, Mommy?"

Faith nodded but made no verbal reply.

"I think I'd like to have him for my new daddy."

"When and if the Lord wants you to have a new *daed*, He will let us know."

Melinda grinned at her. "I think my daddy went away so Noah could come."

"Honey, you shouldn't be talking that way."

"Why not?"

"Yeah, Faith. Why not?" Susie chimed in.

A vision of Noah's face popped into Faith's mind. She did care for him, but was that enough? Could she trust him not to hurt her, the way Greg had? Did Noah care about her in any way other than friendship? She had so many unanswered questions.

For a while, Faith had thought Noah might have some romantic interest in her, but here of late, he'd pulled back. She figured he must have some reservations about becoming involved with a woman who didn't share his strong faith in

God. Or maybe it was their age difference that bothered him.

Faith shook her head, trying to clear away the thoughts. From what she'd come to know about Noah, she doubted he would see the few years between them as a problem. It was probably her lack of faith that concerned him the most. She reached over and pulled Melinda into her arms.

"What's wrong, Mommy? How come you're cryin'?"

"Mine are the good kind of tears, sweetie. Tears of joy."

"What are you so happy about?" Susie questioned.

Faith hugged both little girls. "I'm thankful to God for giving me you two. I'm also happy to be back here in Webster County, and this is where I plan to stay." She turned toward the living room. "Now I must speak to Grandma Stutzman. She needs to know what I've decided."

❧

The next Sunday during Preaching, Noah couldn't help but notice Faith, who sat across the room on the women's side. Something about her expression drew him. Her peaceful look made him wonder if she'd had a personal encounter with God. Could it be? Dare he hope for such a miracle?

Noah kept watching Faith. She sat up straight and seemed to be listening to everything the bishop said. Every once in a while, she blew her nose or dabbed the corners of her eyes with her handkerchief. Noah couldn't wait for church to end so he could talk to her.

After the service was over, tables were set up in the barn for the men and boys. The women and girls would be eating inside the house today. Noah was disappointed when Faith wasn't one of the servers at his table, but he figured he would probably get the chance to speak with her after the meal. That chance never came, though. His mother had taken ill shortly after they were finished eating. She let Noah and his dad know right away, and Pap thought it best if they went on home. Since Noah had ridden to Preaching with his folks that morning, he had no choice but to leave when they did.

As he drove the buggy home, with his parents in the back seat, Noah prayed.

Lord, I'm suspectin' there's been a change in Faith's heart. I don't know if that means she'll be receptive to the idea of me and her courtin', but I'd sure like the opportunity to speak with her about it. I'll go over to the Stutzmans' as soon as I get the chance, and I'm leavin' it in Your hands as to how things will turn out. It's time to learn where Faith stands spiritually, and I plan to reveal my true feelings to her, even if it means rejection.

seventeen

It was February already, and Noah still hadn't spoken with Faith. Since Mom wasn't feeling well yet, he'd gone straight home after work every evening, and his Saturdays were spent cleaning house, cooking, and helping Pap with some of the outside chores.

Today was one of those busy Saturdays, and Noah had spent the entire morning baking bread and one of his famous Lemon Sponge pies. Mom was having a better day, so he hoped to drive over to the Stutzmans' after their noon meal, while his mother took a nap. Pap had announced his intentions to go visit his friend Vernon, the buggy maker. It would be the perfect time for Noah to slip away, and since he'd been praying for Faith instead of pushing, Noah felt confident it would be within God's will for him to make this call.

❧

Faith couldn't believe she and Melinda had the whole house to themselves. Her folks had gone to Seymour for the day, and they'd taken Grace, Esther, and Susie with them. John and Brian were over at their friend Andy's house, so it would be a good opportunity for Faith to work on her baking skills.

She'd thought Melinda might help her make a Lemon Sponge pie, but the child acted sleepy after eating their noon meal and had gone to the living room to take a nap on the sofa.

"It's probably just as well," Faith murmured, as she took out the necessary ingredients to make the pie. Melinda had stayed up late last night, complaining of a tummy ache, and Faith figured a nap would do the child more good than playing in dusty flour and lemon filling.

If the pie turned out well, Faith planned to give it to Noah. He'd presented her with so many special treats over the last few months; it was the least she could do to reciprocate. He'd been kind in other ways, too—helping out when it was needed and sharing God's Word with her on several occasions.

Faith was sure those verses of scripture had taken root in her soul, but it wasn't until the day she'd discovered Melinda yodeling in the barn that she'd really given her heart to Jesus.

As Faith busied herself with the pie making, she smiled at the remembrance of telling Mama she'd changed her mind about leaving. The two of them had sat on the sofa, holding each other and weeping for all they were worth. Mama promised to be more accepting of Faith and her jokes, and Faith said she'd try not to act silly at inopportune times. She'd even had a talk with Papa later that day, and he said he was right glad to have her back home.

Everything's better here now, Faith mused, *but I still have some unfinished business with Noah.*

She put her thoughts on hold and focused on the pie again. When it was ready to bake, Faith discovered the oven wasn't. It didn't seem hot enough. During the summer months, the Stutzmans often used their propane stove, but in the wintertime, Mama insisted on the wood-burning stove because it gave off more heat and circulated throughout much of the house.

Faith slipped the pie onto the oven rack and opened the firebox door. Then she grabbed two pieces of wood from the nearby container and tossed them in. During the process, one of the burning logs inside the stove rolled out and landed on the floor.

She gasped as she watched the braided throw rug ignite. She'd never dealt with a situation like this and wasn't sure what to do. With a shrill scream, Faith slammed the firebox door and tore out of the room. Melinda! She had to get her daughter out of the house.

Thankful the child was downstairs and not up, Faith rushed into the living room. She scooped Melinda up and bounded out the back door into the cold afternoon air.

By this time, Melinda was wide-awake. "Mommy, what's going on? Why are we outside with no coats?"

Faith seated her daughter on a bench at the picnic table and drew in a deep breath to steady her nerves. *Think. I need to think.*

She closed her eyes and offered up a brief prayer. *Dear Lord, tell me what to do.*

When she opened her eyes again, Faith felt a sense of calm. "I caught the rug on fire in the kitchen," she explained to Melinda. "You stay here, and I'll be right back."

"Mommy, where are you going?"

"Stay put!"

❧

It was a fine afternoon, and Noah enjoyed the open sleigh ride over to the Stutzmans'. Even though the air was frosty and snow covered the ground, the sky was a clear blue, with the sun shining bright as a new penny.

Noah glanced at the pie sitting on the seat beside him. He could hardly wait to give it to Faith and have a little heart-to-heart chat. He hoped he would find her at home and also hoped they'd have the chance to talk in private. The words he had in his heart were for Faith's ears alone, and he knew if her family were around, someone would probably be listening in on the conversation.

When Noah pulled into the Stutzmans' driveway, his heart lurched. Melinda was sitting at the picnic table with her arms wrapped tightly around her middle. What was Faith thinking, letting her daughter play out in the snow with no coat?

He grabbed the pie, hopped down from the buggy, and was approaching Melinda when he noticed a chunk of smoldering wood and what looked like the remains of a throw rug lying in the snow several feet from the house.

Melinda jumped up and raced over to Noah. "It's so good you're here. I'm worried about Mommy."

Noah's heart began to pound, and then he saw it—smoke drifting out the back door of the Stutzmans' home.

"Where is she, Melinda? Where's your *mamm*?"

The child pointed toward the house, her lower lip quivering like a leaf in the wind.

The reality of what the smoldering log and burned throw rug meant caused Noah to shudder. "Stay here, Melinda." He handed her the pie. "I'm goin' inside to help your mother."

Noah took the steps two at a time, and when he bounded into the smoke-filled kitchen, he was thankful he saw no flames. "Faith! Where are you?"

Through the haze of smoke, he noticed a moving shadow, and he reached for it. What he got was a wet towel slapped against his arm. "Hey! What's goin' on?"

"Noah, is that you?" Faith stepped through the stifling fog, waving the towel in front of her.

Relieved to see she was all right and with barely a thought for what he was doing, Noah grabbed her in a hug. "Are you okay? What happened in here?"

Faith coughed several times. "I was trying to do some baking, and the oven wasn't hot enough. When I opened the firebox, a log rolled out and caught the braided rug on fire." She leaned into him. "My first thought was to get Melinda outside; then I came back in here to be sure the fire hadn't spread and to dispose of the rug."

Noah's heart clenched at the thought of what could have happened if Faith hadn't thought quickly enough. The whole house might have burned to the ground, the way his dad's barn had when it was struck by lightning.

"Where're your folks and the rest of the family?" he asked, stroking Faith's back.

She coughed again and pulled slowly away, leaving him with a sense of disappointment. "They're all gone for the day. Only me and Melinda are here, and I was trying to bake you a Lemon Sponge pie." Her voice quavered, and she gasped. "Oh no! My pie! It must be burned to a crisp."

She threw open the oven door and withdrew the pie. Even in the smoky room, Noah could see it was ruined.

Faith groaned and set the blackened dessert on the counter. "I can't believe what a mess I've made of things. It seems I can never do anything right."

"It's okay," he said. "It's the thought that counts. Besides, I brought you a Lemon Sponge pie I made this morning. I left it outside with Melinda." Now it was Noah's turn to cough. Between the firebox being left open and the burned pie, there was a lot of smoke. "We need to get this room cleared out. Let's open some windows and head outside."

Soon they had the doors and windows open, and Noah had taken Melinda and Faith to the barn where it was warmer. Noah noticed how Faith's eyes were brimming with tears, and he wasn't sure if it was from the acrid smoke or because she was upset over the frightening incident. Probably a little of both, he decided.

Relief flooded his soul as he stared down at Faith and her daughter, sitting side by side on a bale of straw. He reached for Faith's hand, and she stood. He wanted to kiss her. His chest rose and fell in a deep sigh. "Faith."

❧

From the look of desire she saw in Noah's dark eyes, Faith was fairly certain he wanted to kiss her. She leaned forward slightly, inviting him to do so, but to her disappointment, he moved away. Had she misread his intentions? This was the man she'd come to love. She could hardly bear the thought he might not love her in return.

She rubbed her hands briskly over her arms, trying to calm her racing heart. "I could have burned the house down today, but the Lord was watching out for me—for all of us really."

"*Jah*, I believe you're right about that, but I'm kinda surprised to hear you sayin' so."

She touched his arm. "I'm not an unbeliever, Noah. I recently asked God to forgive my sins, and I'm believing He will strengthen my faith as time goes on."

A slow smile spread across Noah's face. "Really, Faith?"

She nodded.

"That's *wunderbaar!*"

"I'm not leaving Webster County, either," she said with a catch in her voice.

"Had you been plannin' to?"

She nodded soberly. "Yes, but God changed my mind."

"I've suspected you were thinkin' about going."

She hung her head. "From the beginning, I'd planned to leave Melinda with my folks and head back on the road again."

"You were gonna leave me here?"

Faith spun around at the sound of her daughter's voice. She'd forgotten Melinda was within earshot. What had she been thinking? She hadn't wanted Melinda to know.

She swept the child into her arms. "Honey, I'm so sorry. I thought it would be best for you, but God kept causing things to happen so I'd have to stay put."

Melinda sniffed deeply. "You're not leavin' then?"

"No. My place is here with you."

"And you won't be tellin' jokes and yodelin' no more?"

Before Faith had a chance to answer, Noah cut in. "I think it would be fine if your *mamm* kept tellin' her funny stories and jokes right here with her family, don't you?"

Melinda nodded and swiped at the tears rolling down her cheeks. "Will ya still be able to yodel, Mommy? I love it when you do."

Faith smiled through her own set of tears. "I don't think most see yodelin' as wrong, but I probably won't do it when Grandpa Stutzman's around. I'm pretty sure it bothers his ears."

Noah chuckled. "Well, he ain't here now, so let's have us a little hoedown.

She nodded and squeezed Melinda's hand. "How about if you help me yodel?"

Melinda leaned her head back and opened her mouth. "Oh—lee—dee—ee—oh—lee—dee—tee!"

Noah clapped as they yodeled; then suddenly, he stopped, and his expression was so serious Faith was afraid she'd said or done something wrong.

Noah looked deeply into her eyes. "I love you, Faith Stutzman, and if you think you could learn to love me, I'd like the chance to court you."

Melinda jumped up and down. "Yippee! I knew it!"

Faith swallowed and squeezed her eyes shut. "Oh, Noah, I don't have to *learn* to love you, for I already do. Thanks to God's love and His showing me what's really important, I know I can have the best of both worlds—the love of a wonderful man—and my family and friends—and, most of all, a closeness to my heavenly Father that I've never had before."

He smiled at her. "And you can still keep usin' your talents. Just as I make pies and other baked goods to help folks feel better, you can tell jokes and silly stories that will make 'em laugh." He lifted Faith's chin with his fingertips and lowered his head. Their lips touched, and Faith was sure she'd fallen into a deep sleep and was dreaming the most wonderful dream. It seemed as though God had created their arms to hold one another and their lips to share this special moment.

epilogue

Two years later

Faith brushed Noah's arm with her elbow as she squeezed past him to get to the stove. Two more Lemon Sponge pies were ready to be taken from the oven. These would be given to Barbara and David Zook, in honor of their son, Zachary, who had been born the week before.

"I can't believe we've been doin' this for almost two years," Noah said as he nuzzled Faith's neck with the tip of his nose.

She giggled and glanced down at the floor, where their one-year-old son, Isaiah, was being entertained by his big sister, Melinda.

"God has been good and blessed our marriage," Faith said.

"*Jah*, that's so true."

"What verse of scripture have you decided to attach to one of these pies?" she asked.

"I was thinkin' maybe Luke 16:10. 'He that is faithful in that which is least is faithful also in much.' "

"Sounds like a good one." Faith grabbed a pen and paper off the counter. "Think I'll add a couple of funny quips on one side, and you can put the Bible verse on the other."

Noah nodded. "We make a *gut* team, *Fraa*. Sure glad you decided to marry me."

Faith wrapped her arms around Noah's neck and kissed his cheek. A few tears slipped under her lashes and splashed onto Noah's blue cotton shirt. "I thank the Lord for bringin' me back here two years ago. Home is where my heart is. Home is where I belong."

RECIPE FOR NOAH'S LEMON SPONGE PIE

½ cup sugar
1 tablespoon cornstarch
1 lemon (juice and grated rind)
2 eggs (separated)
1 cup water
1 rounded tablespoon butter
Pinch of salt

Line a pie tin with pastry and bake in 350° oven until crust is golden brown. Mix egg yolks, cornstarch, water, sugar, and butter. Cook together over boiling water in top of double boiler, stirring constantly until thick and smooth. Cool. Add lemon juice, grated rind, and salt to stiffly beaten egg whites. Stir this mixture into the cooled custard. Spread in baked pie shell.

Top with meringue, made from 2 stiffly beaten egg whites and 3 tablespoons confectioner's sugar. Heap meringue lightly on the pie and bake in 350° oven about 15 minutes or until meringue is golden brown.

Turn off heat, wedge oven door open a little, and let pie cool slowly in cooling oven. Makes one 8-inch pie.

A Letter To Our Readers

Dear Reader:

In order that we might better contribute to your reading enjoyment, we would appreciate your taking a few minutes to respond to the following questions. We welcome your comments and read each form and letter we receive. When completed, please return to the following:

Fiction Editor
Heartsong Presents
PO Box 719
Uhrichsville, Ohio 44683

1. Did you enjoy reading *Going Home* by Wanda E. Brunstetter?
   ❏ Very much! I would like to see more books by this author!
   ❏ Moderately. I would have enjoyed it more if
   _____
   _____
   _____

2. Are you a member of **Heartsong Presents**? ❏ Yes ❏ No
   If no, where did you purchase this book? _____
   _____

3. How would you rate, on a scale from 1 (poor) to 5 (superior), the cover design? _____

4. On a scale from 1 (poor) to 10 (superior), please rate the following elements.

   ____ Heroine   ____ Plot
   ____ Hero   ____ Inspirational theme
   ____ Setting   ____ Secondary characters

5. These characters were special because?_____

_____

_____

6. How has this book inspired your life?_____

_____

_____

7. What settings would you like to see covered in future
   Heartsong Presents books? _____

_____

_____

8. What are some inspirational themes you would like to see
   treated in future books? _____

_____

_____

9. Would you be interested in reading other **Heartsong
   Presents** titles? ❑ Yes ❑ No

10. Please check your age range:
   ❑ Under 18   ❑ 18-24
   ❑ 25-34   ❑ 35-45
   ❑ 46-55   ❑ Over 55

Name _____

Occupation _____

Address _____

City_____ State_____ Zip_____

Sweet Treats

4 stories in 1

*T*hese four complete novels follow the culinary adventures—and misadventures—of Cynthia and three of her culinary students who want to stir up a little romance.

Four seasoned authors blend their skills in this delightful compilation: Wanda E. Brunstetter, Birdie L. Etchison, Pamela Griffin, and Tamela Hancock Murray.

Contemporary, paperback, 368 pages, 5 ³/₁₆" x 8"

❤ ❤ ❤ ❤ ❤ ❤ ❤ ❤ ❤ ❤ 💖 ❤ ❤ ❤ ❤ ❤ ❤ ❤ ❤ ❤

❤ ❤ ❤ ❤ ❤ ❤ ❤ ❤ ❤ ❤ 💖 ❤ ❤ ❤ ❤ ❤ ❤ ❤ ❤ ❤

Presents

Great Inspirational Romance at a Great Price!

Heartsong Presents books are inspirational romances in contemporary and historical settings, designed to give you an enjoyable, spirit-lifting reading experience. You can choose wonderfully written titles from some of today's best authors like Hannah Alexander, Andrea Boeshaar, Yvonne Lehman, Tracie Peterson, and many others.

When ordering quantities less than twelve, above titles are $2.97 each.
Not all titles may be available at time of order.

SEND TO: **Heartsong Presents** Reader's Service
P.O. Box 721, Uhrichsville, Ohio 44683

Please send me the items checked above. I am enclosing $ _____
(please add $2.00 to cover postage per order. OH add 7% tax. NJ add 6%.). Send check or money order, no cash or C.O.D.s, please.

To place a credit card order, call 1-800-847-8270.

NAME _____

ADDRESS _____

CITY/STATE _____ ZIP_____